DARK CREATURES

THE DARK CREATURES SAGA - BOOK 1

ELLA STONE

ALSO BY ELLA STONE

Dark Creatures Prequel Novellas

Mother of Wolves

Son of a Vampire

Man and Wolf

Call of the Grimoire

The Dark Creatures Saga

Dark Creatures

Dark Destiny

Dark Deception

Dark Redemption

Dark Reckoning

The Bloodsuckers Blog Series

Life Sucks

Love Bites

Lost Souls

This story is a work of fiction. All names, characters, organisations, places, events and incidents are products of the author's imagination or are used fictitiously. Any resemblance to any persons, alive or dead, events or locals is entirely coincidental.

Text copyright © 2021 Ella Stone

First published 2021

Darkerside Publications

ISBN: 9798451180969

Edited by Carol Worwood

Cover design by Christian Bentulan

All rights reserved.

No part of this book should be reproduced in any way without the express permission of the author.

PROLOGUE

I step towards him again. There's no fear now, just certainty. I am going to die, tonight, here, in this room, staring into the eyes that have haunted me for a decade. There's nothing left to be afraid of.

"You can tell me the truth," I say, so close to him that I can see the sharp points of his fangs. See the dark abyss of his pupils. "We know it will never leave this room. I deserve the truth, at least. Tell me. Why did you kill him?"

He steps closer and raises a hand. His ice-cold fingers caress the side of my neck and I stifle a gasp. A stray tear weaves its way down my cheek.

"As you wish."

I hold my breath, waiting for the last words I will ever hear.

1

Narissa

I have done a lot of stupid things in my life but, I'm willing to bet, this one tops them all.

Pulling my jacket tighter around my chest, I bounce on the spot against the cold, as I glance down and check the time on my watch. 8:15 p.m. Two minutes on from the last time I looked. Four minutes since the time before that. There's a pattern emerging here. It's just nerves. I know that. Rational nerves, but nerves nonetheless. After all, if this goes south, there is more at stake than my one-and-only remaining friendship.

Don't worry, you've got this, I say to myself, my eyes scanning up and down the road. *This is going to work.*

I'm not sure if the pep-talk helps. I'm not a pep-talk sort of person. I'm the sort of person who rolls their eyes at pep-talks and tells people to get the hell on with it.

Still, it means I'm not staring at my watch and debating the stupidity of what I'm about to do. I'm pretty sure if anyone had any idea what I was about to face, they'd say I was suicidal. But I'm not. I know the risks. I'm just out of options.

In some parts of the city, people would cast either a disgusted or amorous eye at a twenty-four-year-old student, standing at the curb in ripped jeans and a cropped jacket at this time of evening. In lots of parts, actually. But this isn't that type of area. This is a nice part of London. This is Mayfair. Hyde Park just a few roads away. Here, the houses are as big as museums and have tiny little balconies with trees in pots. Small trees obviously, but all perfectly pruned to the same shape and size. They could be plastic, I suppose, but I bet they're not. I bet, when you've got enough money to live in a place like this, you pay people to give your trees a daily manicure.

The fact that he's living here means he's got money. And, if he's got money, he's likely to know things. And that's what I need right now. I wouldn't be taking this risk for some bottom-rung vampire.

I pull a crumpled piece of paper from my pocket and stretch it flat, scanning the information there, but conveniently ignoring the name of the recipient at the top of the printout. A name which is not mine. In fact, mine isn't any of the three which appear on this document. Guilt trickles through me. If it did get back to Blackwatch that I'd pulled this off, Oliver would probably end up in a whole heap of shit and, of all the people in the world I don't want to get into shit, he is at the top of the list. Then again, if he'd just helped me when I asked him to, I wouldn't have been forced to resort to stealing.

Taking a deep breath in, I check the time, date and address again, (the time on the paper, as opposed to that on my watch, for once.) I've definitely got the date and address right. As for the time, I'm early. But that's good. The notes on the printout say to arrive early and let myself in. Hopefully, that will give me a little extra time for snooping too.

I'm about to check my watch again, when I spot her across the road, and something in my chest does a full-on flip. She's dressed perfectly for this part of town, in a long, powder-blue, double-breasted coat, and her hair is pinned up in a half-formal manner. But her shoes are scuffed and she keeps throwing glances over her shoulder, like she's terrified someone is watching her. Which I am. But that's not the point. I'm not one of them. And I doubt she even knows what they are yet.

"Joanna?" I dart across the road and block her path. "It is Joanna Castle, isn't it?"

She stops abruptly, her eyes widening as she casts yet another petrified look around her.

"Who are you? Are you with them? Are you one of the ones who sent me?"

"Blackwatch?" I ask.

Her eyes fall to the piece of paper in my hand. As quickly as possible, I scrunch it into a ball and shove it back into my pocket.

"No, I'm not with them. Well, not officially. I'm here to make you a proposition."

A furrow forms between her eyebrows. "I thought that was why I was here? I thought… This is my first time doing this. They said I would understand what to do when I got here."

The guilt I felt for stealing from Oliver is immediately swept away. This poor girl doesn't have a clue what she's walking into. Not the foggiest. My best guess is that Blackwatch picked her off some dodgy street corner, offered her ten times her usual fee and she gets to keep her legs shut, as long as she keeps her mouth shut too. No sex, but she'll still be selling herself. Just a different part.

"Look," I say. "I know they don't tell you much, but you've got to believe me. This place they're sending you to, it's not somewhere you want to go. It's not a job you want to do."

She snorts. "Yeah, like I need you to tell me that. You think anyone wants to do this sort of thing? But I need the money." Her eyes meet mine. "I really need the money."

I can tell. It's not just the scuffed shoes. Up close, her cheeks are sunken, her skin is sallow and the makeup has only gone so far as to cover the blue-grey rings around her eyes. A twinge of sympathy catches me by surprise, and I reach out and take her hand. "Look, I get it. I do. But you've got to trust me. These ... things. They aren't like your normal clients. They aren't... normal."

Her lips begin to tremble. "Like I said, there's nothing I can do. I need the money."

As she turns to go, I hold onto her hand. "Joanna, listen. Let me go up there. We can split the money, fifty-fifty. You don't want to do this."

"And you do?" Her eyebrows rise quizzically, a hardness now fixed in her expression.

"No, not particularly, but I'm better prepared. I know what I'm getting into." I pause for a minute to give my words some time to sink in. "Look, I'm betting fifty percent of what you get for this is still equivalent to half a week's regular work, right? And, this way, there's no risk involved."

While her eyebrows remain raised, a deep furrow etches its way between them.

"What do you get out of this?" she asks. "If this guy is as bad as you claim, why would you risk going up there?"

It's a good question, and one I can't give an honest answer to. But I try to stay as close to the truth as I can manage.

"For closure," I say.

She immediately shakes her head. "No way. Those guys—Blackwatch was it?—they know I'm here. They sent me here. If you go in there and stir up something... if you, you know ..."

"Oh God, no." I lift up my hands, realising what she thinks my plan is. "I'm not going to hurt him. I don't think I even could. I just need to talk to him, that's all. I promise. Nothing bad is going to come from this if you let me go up there. I just need to speak to him."

And then, as if she understands on some level—even though there's really no way she can—she nods.

"Sixty-forty?"

I try to look peeved. As it happens, I am in need of a cash injection myself, but I'd go up there for nothing. Besides, I know what she's getting paid.

"Fine." I say, offering a hand to shake, which she reluctantly accepts.

A flood of relief washes through me. Finding a printout in Oliver's home office had taken weeks of snooping about, sending him out on pizza runs and suggesting the most boring, tedious films possible to watch, in the hope he would fall asleep, so I could duck into his room for a rummage about. If this hadn't panned out, I would be back to skulking in tube stations and dodgy bars.

"He messaged me earlier," Joanna says, pulling her phone out of her baby-blue coat. "The client that is. There's a code for the door. Here."

She turns the screen to me, where I read the message and lock the four-digit number away in my memory. 1891. If I were to hazard a guess, I'd say it's a date of birth. His probably. Even dead people are predictable.

"This is me," I say, now typing my number into her phone. "Call me now, so I have your number too. Then, when I'm done, I'll call you and give you your share of the money."

A brief moment of hesitation flickers across her face. "Just to be clear, you're not going to … you know … do anything that would get me in trouble, right? You promise?"

There's a split second of silence. One that engulfs us so completely, I can almost hear her heart beating. Mine too. A hundred images flash through my head. Memories that I've spent the last ten years trying to shut away. Memories that cause my chest to sear with pain and my pulse to ratchet up so hard, it feels it could actually crack a rib. Yet, when I look back at the girl, my face is a picture of calm. After all, in a city of ten thousand vampires, what's the chance that this is the one I'm hell bent on killing?

"No. Of course not." I offer my best smile. "All I want to do is talk."

2

My good mood is dampened as I enter the building, wearing the blue, woollen coat. This thing is as itchy as hell. No joke. It's no wonder rich women always look so damn miserable all the time, if their wardrobe makes them feel like this. They should invest in some silky-smooth polyester. Still, it was a good call on Joanna's part. I was only six feet from the entrance, when she called me back.

"Wait," she'd said, coming over to me and pulling off the coat. "The man who … who found me. The Blackwatch man. He said I should dress nicely for this. You know …" she'd looked me up and down, "… classy."

I'm sure a lesser person would have reacted to the blatant insult in both the comment and the look. To be honest, I hadn't really thought about the appropriateness or otherwise of my attire when I got dressed this morning. Or any morning for the last decade for that matter. Jeans, an old T-shirt and trainers in summer. Jeans, a jumper and boots in winter. With a wardrobe as extensive as that, you can't go wrong. You're sorted for anything: work, lectures, social situations. Okay, scrap the social situations part. I wasn't exactly a social butterfly before everything happened. Now, I'd be deemed a borderline recluse. If I didn't have to do things like attend lectures and earn money, (another little problem I've chosen to throw on the back burner), I doubt I'd even leave the house. Anyway, I guess what I was saying is that it was a good call on the girl's part. There was no way Blackwatch would have let me go to a client dressed like I was, so the coat was a good idea. Although it's probably not going to stay on that long, once I'm in there.

Even from the outside, you can tell the building is dripping with money. It's one of those places with sash windows and an enormous, elaborate, stone archway over the door. Inside, and beyond the stairs in the lobby, is a lift with an iron grille. Seriously. A full-on lift. Stepping inside, I slide the metal door shut and take a second to steady my breathing. According to the instructions on Oliver's sheet, this thing lives on the third floor, so that's the button I press. For the next thirty seconds, the floors slide slowly by on the other side of the ironwork. With a sudden lurch, the lift stops and I soon find myself on the landing, staring at a big, lone, wooden door. This would be me.

Just as Joanna had said, there is a keypad positioned by the front door and it only takes a moment to type in the number. I'm in a hurry to get as much snooping done as possible, before he arrives, although when the light turns green and the door clicks open, I lose a minute just standing and gawping.

"Jesus."

From the typical, classical styling of the building's outside, I'd expected the same of the apartment inside, but this place could be something out of a James Bond film.

As much as I hate to admit it, I guess my stereotypes when it comes to vampires are pretty ingrained and, as I step inside, I realise that I had been expecting something far more gothic. Velvet curtains, perhaps. Maybe a few candlesticks and chandeliers, or paintings of serious-looking men, with cravats, staring down from the walls. I realise that's profiling but, when you drink people's blood to survive, you lose the right to be offended.

Whilst it's definitely no basement crypt, the place isn't exactly homely. I guess you'd call it a studio flat, in the sense that it's open plan, but it is easily twice as big as any flat I've ever lived in. My eye is drawn to the kitchen area, which I'm willing to bet has never been used. The countertops there are of gleaming, black marble, in stark contrast to the brilliant-white cupboards. Only the wooden floor, varnished the colour of honey, offers any warmth. Curiosity gets the better of me and I make my way around to the fridge and open it. Disappointingly, I find it only contains a couple of bottles of soda water.

"Interesting," I say, locking that little detail away. Maybe there's something significant about it. Maybe soda water offers some kind of natural repellent to holy water. Not that that actually works, according to my dad. My dad. The reason I'm here. The only reason I know these things exist. And the reason I want revenge.

With the fridge closed again, I open a couple of drawers. The cutlery is spookily clean and obsessively straight, like it's never been used. Which is probably the case. Still, I'm careful not to disturb anything. It doesn't take me long to get bored looking in the show-home cupboards, so instead, I move over to the bed. I don't know anything about thread count or organic cotton, but even I can tell this is expensive material. Seriously expensive. Dark blue. Super soft, I notice, as I run my hand over it, only to leave a massive crease across what had previously been a perfectly made bed.

"Shit."

I try and smooth it out again, only to make matters worse. I know this sounds lame, but I'm rubbish at making beds. I really am. I could blame it on the fact that I lost my mum when I was young, but my dad was awesome at it. So maybe it's his fault. Maybe I never bothered to learn properly, because he was so good at it. That was certainly the case with cooking. God, I miss his cooking. I miss all of him. Even his crappy jokes. And he'd know so much about this freak, just by stepping in here. Hell, he might even know who the guy is. But Dad isn't here. That's why I am. That's why I've got to do everything I can to make them pay for what they did to him. I can feel heat starting to prick at my eyes. I try to shake the memories away and distract myself by snooping through the wardrobe. The selection of clothes inside is predictably monochrome.

"I see you've been making yourself at home?"

Spinning around, I force myself to stifle a gasp.

"Well don't."

3

It was the shock that made me want to scream. Just like I would if anyone had jumped out at me, in what I'd assumed was an entirely empty flat. My instinct is to reach for my back pocket, and the pencil-thin stake that's in there, but once I've composed myself, which I think I do pretty damn fast considering, I realise there's good news and there's bad news. The good news is, he doesn't lunge straight for my throat. The bad news is, he's not the one I'm looking for.

I guess, deep down, I knew that would be the case. Still, I was hoping it would be that easy. Just like I'd hoped with all the seedy bars jobs I took that one day he might stumble into one of them. Or all the nights I traipsed tube station after tube station, searching in the shadows most people would steer clear of. But that's why I came here. To get information. And now, whether I want to or not, I'll have to see this plan through.

"Joanna, isn't it?" he asks, his eyes fixed on me, as he takes off his jacket.

I nod, pulling my own coat tighter around me. His gaze stays on me for a second longer and I'm convinced he knows I'm lying, but then he turns and hangs his jacket on a hook by the door.

"Blackwatch said you're new to this. Is that true?"

I nod again. I'm still not sure what angle I'm going to play here. Threatening him won't get me anywhere. Seduction could be an option but, then again, maybe this one doesn't like to play with his food. I opt for casually terrified. It's what I feel Joanna would have been. Besides it is, at this precise moment, one hundred percent true.

"I'll need to freshen up."

With his jacket gone, he starts to unbutton his shirt and moves towards a door I assume to be the bathroom. As his hand touches the handle, he turns back to me. "And if you can leave the bed alone and sit on the sofa, it would be greatly appreciated."

A second later, he's gone. *Prick.* I think it to myself, careful not to mutter things under my breath, given their acute hearing. Still, who talks like that? *"It would be greatly appreciated."* You know what I'd greatly appreciate? If every one of his fucking kind was eradicated from the planet. And, since the chances of that happening are slim, I'm going to settle on just killing the one who ruined my life.

When he returns from the bathroom, the shirt is gone, and he's wearing a tight, black T-shirt with his jeans. There's a small possibility my eyes are drawn to the region of his abdominals but, let's be serious, it can't be hard to maintain a figure like that when all you drink is blood. No late-night pizza deliveries. No cheeky kebabs on the way home after a late shift. And I know—

according to Dad and Oliver, at least—that these guys do sleep. But I doubt they *sleep* sleep, like we do. I mean, screw eight hours, I'm a girl who'll say yes to fourteen if you'll let me have them. While, between studying and attempting to earn some money, I haven't seen the inside of a gym in an age, that's not a problem for this guy. He's got eternity. Literally. So, yes, I may inadvertently be staring at his abs, but it's only because it makes me hate him even more.

"Can I get you something to drink?" he asks, wiping his hand on his trousers. "I see you've already assessed the contents of my fridge, so you're aware the selection is limited. I can always order something, if you'd like. Or food, if you're hungry."

"I thought that was why I was here?" I say.

His eyes flash. It was meant as a half-hearted attempt at humour and, obviously, it has fallen seriously short.

"They already told you why you are needed here?"

"I ... well ..." I can feel a lump building in my throat, as I work out how to worm my way out of this one. It shouldn't be that hard, I try to remind myself. I've been lying to my friends, on and off, for years. And I study English. Words are my thing. Only, at this precise moment, they are definitely not.

"I've heard rumours," I say, flicking my hair back, like I'm on some freaking telenovela.

"What sort of rumours?"

"You know. Girls like me. Being offered a lot of money to let men like you do certain things to them."

His eyes narrow. I'm almost a hundred percent positive that vampires have no psychic ability whatsoever, but I still can't help feeling that I'm screwed. I'm expecting him to kick me out or, worse still, call Blackwatch and say he wants a change of donor, but then he perches on one of the tall bar stools.

"Well, as I get the impression that niceties are clearly superfluous in this instance, I guess we should just get on with the task at hand."

He gestures to the stool beside him. *Fuck.* It's the only word that goes through my head. The whole point was I wanted him to talk. I need him to tell me about them. I should have pretended to be ignorant and got him to explain as much as possible. How many. Where they hang out. Who the top-level ones are. I should have drawn this out as long as I could, but now I'm actually going to do this. I'm actually going to let this monster feed from me. I feel the air quivering in my lungs. If he's ever going to tell me something that might help me find the vampire I'm after, I need him to trust me. And if losing a few fluid ounces of haemoglobin is what it's going to take, then I guess we're doing it.

I make no attempt to calm myself as I cross the room to sit beside him. He can already hear that I'm terrified. Probably smell it on me too. Good. I don't care what bullshit truce Blackwatch and the vampires have. They may have managed to stay hidden for all of history; they might have managed to pull the wool over Oliver and Jessop and everyone else's eyes. But not mine. I've seen what they can do, first hand. You don't forget something like that. Not ever.

Feeling like I'm about to throw up, I take my place on the stool next to him. My skin is prickling. All the hairs on the back of my neck are rising. Every living cell within me is repulsed by his absence of life. Swallowing it all back down, I flick my hair over my shoulder again, tilting my head, exposing my throat to him. I wait like this, wondering whether I'm going to vomit or pass out first, when he clears his throat.

"Actually, I prefer to use the wrist," he says.

"Oh, okay."

Shifting on my seat, I slip the blue coat off. I could be mistaken, but I swear there's a half-smile on his lips, as I reveal my less-than-classy vest top.

Now certain that vomiting is going to win out, I extend my arm to him. Is this better than the neck? I wonder. I know some feed like this. My dad told me enough to know that much. So, if this one wants to feed from here, so be it. I'd let him draw blood from my knee cap if it meant getting closer to what I want to know. Cradling the back of my wrist with one hand, he traces a line from half way down my forearm to the place where my veins start to show blue-green beneath the skin with the other. I am bracing myself for a bite when, instead, he flicks his hand and a long, dagger-like nail extends about half an inch from his index finger, only millimetres away from my wrist.

"What the hell?" I snatch my hand back and hold it to my chest.

A confused look, almost fearful, sparks in his eyes.

"I'm sorry, I should have explained. From your confidence, I thought you knew what I was. What you were here for."

"You're a vampire, I know that. But fangs. I was expecting fangs. Not some weird dagger-finger thing."

A small smile pulls back on the corners of his lips, but he manages to disguise it with the nod of his head.

"There's venom in a vampire's nail. A mild anaesthetic, that's all. A small scratch will stop the bite hurting quite so much. I assure you, it's of no long-term harm to humans. I assume you are a human?"

It's obviously his attempt at humour now, and he looks at me, expectantly, but I keep my arm exactly where it is, against my chest.

"Nope. No venom," I say.

His eyebrows rise. "It will be more painful without."

"I can cope with pain."

It's true. It's bad enough I've got to let this talking corpse sink its teeth into me. I'm not letting it get me with its vampire venom to boot. I'm don't trust a word he says. Fuck knows what that could do to me. Slowly, I loosen my grip on my arm and shift in towards him.

"No nail," I say.

"Understood."

Without another word he takes my arm again, this time placing both of his hands on the underside. My heart is beating so fast, I'm pretty sure it's doing some permanent damage as he lifts my arm upwards, before lowering his head to meet it. Everything my dad did to protect me, and this is where I've ended up. But it's for him. It's all for him. And when I find the vampire that murdered him, he'll pay with his life. This will all be worth it then. A surge of adrenaline shoots through me as a flash of blinding pain sears up my arm.

4

Holy shitting hell! I scream in my head. It's like a bolt of fire shooting up through my veins. I feel the blood pulsing from me and into his mouth. The skin is burning where his fangs pierced it. I can feel my eyes watering and every muscle is rigid and tense. I don't want to scream. More than anything, I don't want to scream. I don't want him to know how much this is hurting me. But I'm not sure how much more I can take. It's only been a few seconds. I feel my legs trembling. Sucking air in through my nose, I'm about to tell him I can't take any more, when his grip loosens. Silently he sits back and wipes his mouth with the back of his hand.

Bizarrely, the pain stops almost as soon as he withdraws his fangs. Two tiny dots of blood appear on my arm, and I stare at them, as they each swell into pools. Reaching across the worktop, he grabs and tears off a few sheets of kitchen towel and hands them to me.

"It will take a minute or two to stop bleeding. There's

anticoagulant in our saliva that makes it easier for us to feed."

"Like a leech?"

"I suppose you could say that."

Only when I look down do I realise how little time has passed. How little time I was pinned there, his teeth in my veins, his lips on my skin. There's none of the light-headedness that I'd expected. Not even a hint of dizziness. I've felt worse after giving blood in a legitimate donation administered by a trained professional.

"Is that it?" I ask. "Is that all you need?"

"It will satisfy me today," he says matter-of-factly. "I did not wish to take too much from you, given it is your first time and you refused the venom."

"Thank you." The words leave my mouth before I can stop them. He nods in response. There's this weird tension around us, like he's expecting more from me. Maybe he's expecting me to ask questions, or to scream, or to curl up in a ball and cry, or beg, or pray to God. Maybe that's what people do the first time they learn that vampires are real. I don't know. I should have looked into it. But the fact is, I've known for years. Even before I saw one snap my father's neck like a twig. He never hid what he did from me. Some days, I wish he had.

"I shall fetch you your money," he says, rising from his seat. "I assume you find the Blackwatch rate acceptable?"

"It'll do," I say.

I'm impressed with how well I'm playing this. I don't think for a second that he trusts me, but that's fine. I'm happy to play the long game. If I don't get any more from this, at least I've got one vampire name I can tick off the list as not being my father's killer.

Without another word, he goes over to one of the paintings, pressing the wall just below it, to reveal a secret drawer. Another show of trust. This is good. I make a mental note of how he opens and closes it, with a push of his hand. Secret drawers are a perfect place to hide things and I want to know what he's concealing. Although he hasn't made much effort to disguise it, so I doubt there's much in there.

"So, how does this work?" I ask. "Will I come back to you again, or will Blackwatch send me to another vampire?"

"You would be happy to return here?"

He locks his eyes on mine. Blue-grey, like a clear sky reflecting on ice. There's no emotion. Nothing to read. There's none of the impulsiveness I'd expected or the violence I'd encountered that night in the alley. But just because I can't see it, it doesn't mean it's not there, simmering under the surface, waiting to explode and shred my world apart all over again. Still, he's waiting for an answer.

"I would like to come back here," I say, in as innocent a voice as I can muster. "Prefer it, that is, given that I know you. Given that I know I'm safe here." I add the last bit, somehow sensing that's what he needs to hear.

"I have your number from Blackwatch. I will contact you, if I require you." With a nod of his head, he hands me a wad of cash. "You can count it, if you want to check."

I don't. What I want is to get out of here and go for a stiff drink and forget the insanity of what I'm doing.

Besides, I already know this is a guy who considers integrity a number-one personality trait. For a dead guy, that is.

"I'm sure it's fine," I say, picking up the blue coat and shoving the cash in a pocket. "Am I free to go now?"

"Of course, in my house you are always free to come and go as you see fit."

A cold chill runs down my spine.

"Well in that case, until I see you again?" I say and head to the door.

I don't wait for the lift. Suddenly, the thought of an enclosed space, in a house with a vampire, causes my nausea to return. Instead, I head for the stairs, a slow jog at first, and then as fast as my legs will carry me. One, then two steps at a time, then three, until I reach the ground floor, where I run out the front door and across the road. When I reach the other side, the contents of my stomach spill out onto the pavement at my feet.

"Jesus Christ," I say, when it's over, wiping my mouth with the back of my hand. I stay there for a moment, resting my hands on my knees, panting. When I finally manage to push myself upright again, I glance up to the flat. He is standing at the window, watching me. Observing.

"Let the games begin," I whisper.

As a student, there are a few, low-end establishments that suit my budget when I'm in need of a stiff drink, but none of them are around this part of the city. Also, due to an unfortunate incident that occurred a couple of weeks back, stepping foot in any one of those places is likely to see me end up with, at best, a bloody nose or, at worst, a somewhat-extended hospital stay, with countless broken ribs. I'll be fine to go back there in a bit, but it's best I lie low for a couple of months, at least. A drink is high on my list of priorities, but my first port of call, however, is Joanna, where I hand over her share of the money.

"He said he'd contact me, well you, when he next wants to meet. Just let me know, okay? The moment he messages you, forward it straight to me."

Her eyes remained fixed on the cash for a moment longer before she looks up at me with a smile.

"That's fine by me," she says.

Given that my normal haunts are out of bounds and I'm in desperate need of a rum and coke, I head south of the river, to Brixton. Places there come with the advantage of being cheap enough that I'm not going to make too big a dent in tonight's earnings, and no one is currently interested in punching me in the face. The tube is empty, which is good as, every now and again, I find myself lifting up the sleeve on my jacket to look at the bite marks. He's right, they've stopped bleeding, but he didn't mention anything about scarring, or infection. As such, when I hop off the tube, I head to the nearest late-night pharmacy, where I grab a box of plasters and some antiseptic wipes. Do you need to get a jab for a vampire bite? Do I need a tetanus booster? Maybe that's something I can slip into conversation with Oliver, later.

After a short walk, I duck down a set of stairs to a grimy-looking basement bar. There can't be more than half a dozen people in the whole place, and almost every one of them is staring into the distance, or at their phone. No one gives a crap what I'm doing, which is perfect.

"Double rum and coke," I say, taking a seat at the bar and pulling out the wipes and plasters to deal with my arm. It's not exactly the most hygienic of locations to inspect an open wound but hey-ho. The place reeks of smoke which, considering you've not been able to light up in pubs for well over a decade, just goes to show how piss-poor a job they do at cleaning.

"Six-fifty," the barman says, placing a glass down on the coaster in front of me. London prices. I swear, when this is done—when I get that low-life, blood-sucking piece of shit that killed my dad—I'm going to move somewhere it doesn't cost almost an hour's pay to buy a single, freaking drink. Reaching into my pocket, I pull out a note. A fifty.

"Don't you have anything smaller?" the barman asks.

"Just open up a tab. Don't worry, I'll get through it," I say.

Grunting, in a way that's impossible to interpret, he slips the note inside the till, then moves to the other side of the bar, leaving me alone. Which is exactly what I need.

A sigh that carries with it the weight of ten, crappy years, escapes my lips, as I wrap my hands around the glass. Tonight was good, as far as formal introductions into the vampire world go. Fingers crossed, he'll invite me back. He's got no reason not to, after all. I'll be able to start asking him questions next time. Subtly, obviously.

Trying to put the *what-have-beens* and *what-might-bes* out of my head, I lift my drink off the coaster. A second later, the whole thing explodes in my hand. Shards of glass spray upwards, raining down over me and the blue coat.

"What the fuck?"

Spinning around, I find myself face to face with the deepest set of brown eyes you've ever seen. The hairs on my arms stand upright.

"What the hell are you doing here?" I ask, unable to keep the shock out of my voice.

Her smile only widens at my response.

"Hey, Naz. Did you miss me?"

5

The moment continues, for just a split second longer. That face, those eyes. I should be furious. I should kick her arse halfway across London, but I can't. Instead, I shake off the rum and coke mixture from my arms, stand up and wrap them firmly around her in the hardest squeeze I can muster. I want to take it all in.

"What the hell was that in the way of a greeting?" I ask when I finally break away. "You're paying for that drink, you know."

"Sure, why not." She waves her hand to the barman. "Another two of whatever she had. And, obviously, they'll be on the house. You should really invest in more sturdy glassware you know."

"Wait …" I fix my gaze on her. "What the hell are you doing here? How did you find me?"

After what I've seen and been through tonight, the last thing I expected was to be sitting in a bar, grinning like a fool, and yet I can't stop myself. The number of true friends in the city has just doubled, even though it's definitely not a good sign that Rey is back in town.

"Did Blackwatch say you could come back? Does Oliver know you're here?"

"I'm here to see you, among other things. And, in answer to the rest of your questions, no, Blackwatch did not invite me back and, yes, I may have dropped in on Grey earlier."

"And how did he take it?"

"Let's just say agent Grey wasn't quite as amorous as he used to be."

"He's just worried about you. You know he won't tell them."

"Of course I do."

The barman puts down two fresh rum and cokes. Given that my previous seat is now surrounded by bits of glass, we move over to one of the booths. They're better for a private conversation anyway.

"So, you still haven't told me." I say, gulping down half my drink in one pull. "How did you find me? Did you track me here?"

For the first time, her face falls. "No, not even close. Me finding you was nothing but blind luck. I saw you cross the road, although what is it with that blue coat? You know you look ridiculous in it."

"It's a long story," I reply "And, anyway, we're talking about you. You're not meant to be in London. What are you doing? Did you find something out?"

Her lips remain downturned, as she shakes her head. "A full year and all I've got is the same, lousy, party trick. I'm officially the worst witch in the history of existence."

"That's not true," I say. "A year ago, you were the

worst witch in existence. You couldn't do anything. Now you can smash glasses. That's got to have pushed you up a level, right?"

"A year ago, I didn't know I was a witch. Seriously, this is what I got kicked out of Blackwatch for? A fucking parlour trick that any half-decent soprano with a wineglass can manage."

"Then go back to Jessop, tell him that. Tell him he should take you back."

"Sure, march up to the head of the world's primo-shady, supernatural, monitoring agency and say 'Hey, Jessop, I know you fired me for unknowingly concealing the fact I was a witch, but maybe we should just move on.'" Rey sighs. "It's just not going to happen. I know it's not. And I don't have the energy to fight. I just need to find a way to get my hands on some of the grimoire pages."

So that's why she's back. Figures. Grimoires are kept by the vampires. And there are plenty of them in London.

"I assume you asked Oliver," I say, in reference to the grimoires.

"And you can guess how well that went. Still loyal to the cause and screw his friends."

I feel for her, I really do. It's been a decade since my life got turned upside down and I'm nowhere nearer to getting it straight again. It's only been a year for her since she lost everything. Since she found out she's a witch. As Blackwatch can't be associated with witches, due to the fact that vampires are terrified of them and it would pretty much screw up the treaty that's been in place for over two hundred years, they had to kick her out. Blackwatch had been her world. Now she's on her own. No family, no way of tracing her lineage. It can't be fun.

"Now, let's stop moping and talk about more interesting things." Rey forces a grin back onto her face. "Why are you and Grey not shacked up yet?"

I raise my eyebrows in the most sarcastic way I can manage. "You really need to give up on that, you know. Besides, I don't want your cast-offs."

"You know that's not even remotely the case. I just filled a gap while he was pining for you. Ever since you tried to break into Blackwatch, he's been smitten."

"I guess he just has a thing for hopeless causes," I say.

I'm not denying Oliver is a good guy, or anything. He speaks, like, a dozen languages; he's well-mannered; he cleans up after himself; he has a good job—if keeping tabs on vampires can be considered that—and I'm not blind to the fact he is pretty damn hot. I suspect he would be the ideal catch for most women. Personally, all that perfection would be too much for me. I have enough trouble remembering to brush my teeth at night. There's no way I'd be a good match for a person who can give you the past participle for *to go* in almost every European language. I'm suddenly aware of just how long my silence has lasted when Rey comes in with another question.

"Anyway, what are you doing south of the river?" she asks. "And it's a Friday night. Shouldn't you be working at Joe's? I thought you always worked Fridays?"

"Yeah…" I say, elongating the vowel sound, as I raise my glass and focus on the contents. "Let's just say there was a misunderstanding and we parted company."

When I look up from my drink, she's staring straight at me.

"Naz, what did you do?"

"Why would you think I did anything?"

It's her turn to raise an eyebrow.

"I didn't do anything that he didn't deserve."

She blows out a sigh. "How bad? I mean, is he pissed off to the extent that you're not getting a glowing reference, or pissed off to the extent that he's going to come at you with a baseball bat?"

"Probably the second option," I say with a shrug. "But, before that, I was a very good worker. I still think I deserve a decent testimonial."

"How the hell you get yourself into so much shit, I have no idea," she says with a grin.

"I'll drink to that,' I say, lifting up my glass. "To the shit we get ourselves into."

"To the shit we get ourselves into."

Our glasses clink, as we toast ourselves, both of us still grinning like fools. I can't help feeling it's a disaster waiting to happen, Rey turning up like this at the exact moment I manage to find myself a way into the vampire world. Still, if nothing else, it'll make a great story to tell our grandkids when we're old.

Still grinning at the fact that I have my best friend returned to me after a year's absence, I wave to the barman for another round of drinks.

"So, come on then, tell me everything. Where've you been for twelve months? I'm sure you've got plenty to catch me up on."

"Fine, but then you need to tell me what the hell you're doing in that God-awful, blue coat," she says.

6

Between rum and cokes, we while away the hours, although neither of us has much positive news to add to the conversation. Rey, or Andrea Green, has spent the last year travelling the country in search of witches or grimoires, both of which eluded her. Without one or the other, she has no way of learning any more magic. Basically, she's screwed. If she can't learn more, she would have been better off not knowing that she's a witch at all which, deep down, is what she really would have preferred. I feel for her. Honestly, even now, despite the way Blackwatch treated her, I know she'd go back to them at the drop of a hat. Not that that will ever happen, of course.

At times, she turns our conversation back to me and what I'm doing and whether I'm still hunting down Dad's murderer. But it's easy enough to flip it back to her. The advantage of not having seen someone for a year, even if the news they have to tell you isn't very exciting, there's still enough of it to keep you going for a few hours. At ten-to-eleven, the barman calls last orders for us and the two other people slumped over their drinks.

"Okay, where to now?" I ask, as she downs her drink.

"You want to crash at mine? It's not exactly luxurious, but the sofa's all yours, if you want it."

"What have you got in the fridge?"

"My fridge?" I try to think back to the last time I actually opened it. "I've probably got some milk. Cereal. I take it you want food?"

"I do," she replies, a sideways smile slanting upwards. "I want good food. And you know who always has some of that in their fridge, don't you?"

IT'S ONLY BEEN THREE DAYS SINCE I WAS LAST HERE although, on that occasion, I'd turned up under false pretences. I'd been covering my tracks. Exactly a week has passed since I'd snuck into Oliver's office and stolen the details about Joanna's donor appointment. The guilty part of me wishes I could avoid him altogether. But given that I frequently use Oliver's fridge as an all-you-can-eat buffet, I know he'd have been suspicious if I hadn't been round. So, I'd called by on Wednesday, when I knew he'd be at work, stolen some cheese, bread and a can of lager, then left an unwashed plate and the empty can on the kitchen worktop, just so he knew I'd visited. He sent a text later that night, telling me to do my own damn washing up, but I hadn't replied. Still, I guess going to his flat now, with Rey, is a good idea. There's no way I'm going to be able to look him in the eye but, with her there, I might get away with it.

CHAPTER 6

While neither Oliver nor Rey has ever been inclined to divulge their wages at Blackwatch, they must have gone up since my dad was working for them, especially given that she's managed to scour the whole of the UK for the last year without a hint of a pay-cheque, and Oliver has been renting this place for as long as I've known him. It's nowhere near as fancy as the vampire's flat—there's no lift for starters—but it's got two bedrooms and enough space for a pull-out in the living room. There'd be even more room, too, if every wall wasn't covered in bookshelves. Although that's another reason I come here. To steal books. To steal private, classified information. Still, every time I'm here, I can't help but think about my dad and me. Sure, we lived well enough: three square meals a day and a dry roof over our heads but, when he died, there was nothing. No bills and no debts, but no savings. Even his passport had gone by the time I got around to sorting out his things, along with the little, leather notebooks he used to journal in. A piece of him I desperately wish I still had. I guess that's just how Blackwatch likes it—the more invisible they are, the better.

When we knock on the door, Oliver opens it, wearing jeans, a worn, grey T-shirt and a distinct look of disapproval. For a second, I think he's mad at me, then I realise his gaze has gone straight over my shoulder.

"Are you serious? You said you were passing through. Do you have any idea what Jessop would do if he found out you were here?"

"How would he? Are you going to tell him?" Rey pushes her way past me and into the flat, and I follow after her.

"Of course I'm not going to tell him."

"And it's not like Naz is going to say anything, are you Naz?"

"I'm not exactly Jessop's favourite person."

"Precisely. Now, screw the bullshit, I'm desperate for something to eat. What have you got? I fancy grilled cheese. Or scrambled eggs. You've got eggs, right?"

While she gets to work raiding the contents of Oliver's fridge, I slump down on the sofa. For a girl whose average night consists of reading books and occasionally pulling all-nighters to finish essays just hours before their deadline, today has been pretty full on, and the meeting with Joanna feels like days ago. Not to mention the encounter with the vampire; but it feels nice, the three of us back together. Or at least it does until I notice the way Oliver is glaring at me. Even when I pick up the television remote and switch to a comedy channel that I know he hates, he doesn't say a word. An uneasy chill ripples across my skin.

"What?" I ask, without turning to face him, after his creepy, death stare finally gets too much. I feel like I'm going to vomit again. I figure playing innocent is my best bet. At most, he's got his suspicions, although my stomach twists at the thought that maybe he'd got around to installing CCTV, like he always said he would. Still, I stick with the innocent routine.

"Is this about Rey? Because, I swear, I didn't know she was back."

"Nope, this is nothing to do with Andrea." The use of her full name doesn't bode well for either of us, although his face is completely neutral. It's a shame they don't interrogate vampires at Blackwatch. I reckon he'd be awesome at it.

"Have I done something?" I try.

"Why don't you tell me?"

I wrinkle my nose and let my gaze drift up to the ceiling, like I'm actually pondering the question. Finally, I shake my head.

"I'm sorry, I've no idea what you're on about."

"Really? You want to try that? You honestly think I'll fall for that routine?"

Yup, he would be an awesome interrogator. Sweat is starting to form on the back of my neck and I'm pretty sure my knees are trembling. *What's he going to do about it?* I ask myself, trying to rationalise away my panic. I'm ninety-nine percent positive about that he won't tell Jessop and Blackwatch. The only reason I was saved, after I attempted to break into Blackwatch way back when, was because of Jessop's relationship with my dad. I won't get away with that twice. But, given that my friendship with Oliver occurred due to said attempted theft, it would be foolish of him to think I'd changed my ways entirely. So, what does that leave? Him being really pissed off. A few months of silent treatment. I can take that. Still, I'm not going to give in that easily. He might be the master of unblinking, but two can play at that game.

"I *know*, Narissa," he says, without breaking eye contact. "I know what you did. And I've never seen anyone that angry in my life. He said he wants you dead. And I think I believe him. I think you're in trouble this time. Real trouble. I actually believe he does want to kill you."

7

For a solid fifteen seconds, it's like my brain just times out. Nothing. No thinking, no deep whirring, just an absolute blank. Someone wants to kill me? The vampire? Is that who he's talking about? Did mister minimalist discover I was lying about who I said I was and want my blood? No, that makes no sense. He had my blood. He could have killed me there and then, if he'd wanted to. But if not him, then who? Who else wants me dead? Then it all clicks into place.

"Oh, you mean Joe," I say, with genuine relief.

"Yes. I mean Joe."

Obviously, my relief is not that Joe wants me dead. That's not ideal news. It's been a couple of weeks now and if he's still that mad that he's willing to confront Oliver, then there's a good chance he's not going to calm down any time soon. But he doesn't know where to find me and I'm not planning on crossing paths with him, so I'm pretty sure I can ride this one out. Besides, if Oliver is talking about Joe, it means he doesn't know anything about me stealing Joanna's blood-donor information from his office and taking her place. So, all in all, I'd say that's a win.

"You stole from him?" Oliver asks, nailing a look that is somewhere between disappointment and incredulity. (It's hard to believe he never met my dad. The look is almost identical to his.)

"It's hardly stealing. The guy hadn't paid me my full wages for the best part of two years."

"Well, you need to give it back."

"No way. I just told you. I earned that money. Besides, it's gone."

"Gone where?"

Now he's pushing the dad figure way too much. Especially considering he's only a few years older than me.

"Look, I had things to pay for. Tuition. Rent. Books for my course. Stuff I would have been able to afford if he'd not stiffed me on my pay every single week."

"I'm surprised he hasn't broken down the door to your flat to get you."

There's something in the way he emphasises the word *flat*. That's when it clicks into place. The other reason he's so pissed off with me, besides my not telling him about the job situation, and turning up at midnight to raid the contents of his fridge with our supposedly on-the-run friend.

"When exactly were you going to tell me you'd moved?"

"You went to my old place?" I ask, innocently.

"Your *old* place? Yeah, that's right. Just another little thing you forgot to mention?"

This whole interrogation game is getting tedious, but

I guess I'd be pissed off if he pulled the same stunt. Moving house is probably a biggish deal but, in my defence, I didn't think he'd actually be that bothered that I didn't tell him. It wasn't like he visited much. Almost never, really.

"You know I hated it there," I say, slumping back down into the seat. "They're all so young. Partying all the time."

"Oh yes, and I forgot, you're a mature student."

"Yes, I am actually." I say and, to reinforce my point, I stick out my tongue and blow a raspberry at him. At twenty-four, I technically classify as a mature student. However, my behaviour may not always match that description. The truth is that everything that happened with dad meant I really hadn't been in a good mind-set for school. With my mum gone and no other relatives, I bounced around foster homes for a bit, from one house to another. No one cared what I did. That's not to say they were all bad people. Some were, some weren't, but it didn't matter. I was just biding my time until I could exact my revenge. After my exams, I worked one shitty job after another, so I could afford to rent a room. That was when I started tracking vampires in earnest. Back then, it was my every waking thought. Even more so than now. Every second of the day, my mind raced with images of how I'd finally inflict my revenge. Of course, to do that, I actually had to find the guy. After over a year of hopeless dead-ends, I'd attempted to break into the Blackwatch HQ. Jessop was furious when he and Oliver caught me. Like full, purple-in-the-face furious. Instead of yet another of his lectures, he gave me an ultimatum. Forget the vampires and get my life back on track by going to university, or he would turn me over to the cops. Given all those years in foster care, I had enough minor misdemeanours on my record that a run in with the police would probably not end well.

Besides, I'd realised university was a great way of postponing any real form of responsibility for a bit longer, while making him think I'd actually listened to him. It has also offered plenty of time between lectures to focus on some very discreet vampire stalking. On reflection, I'd say it was a win-win decision all round.

"Look," I say, putting on my most mature student voice possible. "I need this year to go well for me. I need to be able to get a good job when I'm done. I can't spend the rest of my life working in shitty little bars. And, let's be honest, half the country has an English literature degree. I need mine to be exceptional. Of course, I wouldn't have to be working quite so hard if I could have got a better-paying job for the last two years. You know, something with shorter working hours. Maybe on a weekly basis. Where the clientele pays over the odds for a little discretion?"

He knows exactly what I'm on about, which isn't really surprising, given that it's probably the most unsubtle hint possible. With a heavy sigh, he picks up the remote from beside me.

"You cannot be a blood donor. You're blacklisted by Blackwatch. You are the *only* person blacklisted by Blackwatch."

"But blood donoring? What could I screw up there? And you have to need more volunteers. My dad always used to say you were short. And I bet there are even more of the fuckers to feed now."

"It's a no, Naz. It'll always be a no."

With a loud huff, I fold my arms across my chest. But, on the inside, I'm definitely smiling. The fact that he fell so seamlessly back into the argument of why I can't be a blood donor, proves one-hundred percent that he has no idea about me taking Joanna's place tonight.

"What are you two talking about?" Rey appears and drops a grilled cheese sandwich in front of me. "How lucky you are that you have me back in your lives? Or have you finally got around to confessing your undying love for one another?"

"Definitely the former," I reply.

"Neither," Oliver says. "I was thinking how much easier my life would be if I moved to some remote, Scottish island."

"Don't you mean how dull?" she asks.

Squeezing herself between us, she picks up the remote and starts flicking through the channels, until she ends up on some reality TV show, where a dozen, obscenely attractive people are placed on a desert island together.

After Oliver and Jessop had caught me breaking in, Jessop had asked him to keep an eye on me. At the time, he and Rey were partners, so they came as a pair, which is something I'll always be grateful for. It's not an exaggeration to say that the two of them have been the only people to really give a shit about me since Dad. More importantly, they are the only people I have given a shit about since him. Despite everything, it's good to be here with them both.

My ability to concentrate on the TV show isn't helped by the fact that the bite mark on my arm feels as itchy as hell. It's screaming out for attention, and every passing minute it's becoming harder and harder not to look at it. I'm struggling to stop myself from fiddling with the plaster which, I'm suddenly aware, is completely on display. I'm now terrified Oliver's going to notice and ask about it. Fortunately, I don't think either he or Rey are thinking much about me. While they were never what you would call a couple, they were also more than just work colleagues. The fact that they haven't seen each other for the best part of a year means they might well be after the type of reunion that would be best served if I wasn't here. So, feigning the most obvious yawn possible, I stretch my arms above my head.

"I ought to head home. Nine a.m. lecture tomorrow," I say.

"You can crash here. You two can take the beds," Oliver suggests, before turning to Rey. "I assume you're staying?"

"See, you did miss me."

"By the most minuscule amount, perhaps."

While they continue their subtle flirting, I stand up and fetch the blue coat from by the door.

"It's fine. If I stay here, I'll have to get up half an hour earlier."

"Do you want me to drop you home?" Oliver never quits easily.

"It's fine, I can get a taxi."

"I'll call you one then," he says and picks up his phone.

"I already called an Uber," I lie, waving my phone at him, to make it look plausible. With my coat on, I wrap my arms around Rey one more time. "I take it you're not going anywhere just yet? We'll catch up again soon."

"Just let me know when you're free, and I'll be there."

"Great, I'll get in touch later."

"Sounds good."

Then I'm out the door, before Oliver can say anything more. It's only when I look at my phone to genuinely call an Uber, that I notice Joanna has forwarded me a text message.

"I would like to see you again tomorrow. Calin."

The vampire. He bought it. I've found my way in.

8

Calin

Hours have passed, and as I step into the shower, the girl remains in my thoughts. She was such a contradiction. So many things about her that didn't make sense. Maybe women are just more complicated these days. Perhaps I'm out of touch. After all, feeding in that manner is not something I choose to do regularly anymore. Not now there are other options available. Blood bags, given to all other vampires, are more than enough to sustain me and the taste, while a little synthetic, is bearable. The issue is that an expectation comes with being a member of the Vampire Council. An expectation that you use the privileges agreed and afforded to you as part of the Blood Pact. So, now and then, to keep up appearances, I request a live feed. And, every time, I dread it. Normally, it is something I push from my mind the moment it's done, but this girl, her taste still lingers.

Memories of my youth—of the inability to control my hunger— flood my mind. It has been decades since I killed someone by mistake. Since the thirst took over and I drained every last drop from a person. But it still isn't something you forget in a hurry. Previous donors I have encountered fall into one of two categories. Either they have been sycophantic groupies, likely aspiring to be turned themselves and deriving an unseemly amount of pleasure from the experience; or scared little rabbits, breaking down in tears or fainting when confronted with the reality of what they have got themselves into. But this girl was different.

I can't quite decide what it was that intrigued me the most. She had shown little surprise or fear at the fact that I was a vampire. Maybe Blackwatch is giving them more information now, although that's unlikely. She said she had heard on the street what she was getting herself into, but that didn't seem to add up, either. Blackwatch pay their donors generously to stop the truth about vampires going public. If there was a leak in their system, they'd probably already know about it. And then to refuse the venom … that was most uncommon.

Switching on the water, I let it cascade over my hair and face, my mind continuing to process the encounter. She was more scared than she'd let on, and lying about something, that much was obvious from the erratic beating of her heart. While we vampires are a long way from being psychic, I had noticed an increase in the rate every time she spoke about herself. Was she on the run, perhaps? It wasn't beyond the realms of possibility. Who knew where Blackwatch found their donors?

Switching the shower off, I pluck a towel from the rail and attempt to shake her from my thoughts.

"You have more than enough to keep yourself busy, without getting fixated on the drama of some girl," I say out loud to myself, as I try to focus on the night ahead and the Vampire Council gathering I have been summoned to.

There again, there's no denying the increase in energy to be gained from a live feed, and Polidori has been on at me to take a more-permanent, live donor for years now. Maybe if I just ask for her one more time. See if I can figure out a little more about this enigmatic girl. I don't have to drink that much.

9

Narissa

Adrenaline's still pumping through my veins when I reach home. En route, I send a text back to Joanna, asking her to arrange a meeting time. Then I message Rey, to see if she's free later in the week. If Blackwatch somehow gets wind that their renegade witch is back in the city, I want to make sure I see her at least one more time before she has to run for it. Who knows, if I manage to hunt down the killer vampire, maybe I'll be fleeing with her.

Arriving at my flat, I kick off my boots and flop onto the sofa. Amazingly, it's only now I realise exactly how exhausted I am. But there's not much point in moving to the bed; it would be no more comfortable there.

I moved into my tiny, basement flat a little over a month ago. Partly so Joe wouldn't know where to find me after I'd liberated the wages he'd owed me and partly because what I said to Oliver about dealing with young, energetic students had actually been true. I am a twenty-four-year-old third year. Putting up with late-night parties and finding random guys sleeping in my bath tub had definitely started to wear thin. Maybe living with some nineteen-year-olds could have been okay if they had been the quiet, bookish types. Girls that liked reading or watching films and occasionally heading to the pub for a quiet pint or two, without feeling the need to put on false lashes and heels. But there had been none of that sort in my old house. They'd acted like they were part of some American sorority, frequently invading my space or searching my wardrobe for anything they could borrow. Not that I'd actually had anything trendy enough for them. I did, however, have plenty of things I'd rather they not find. Sketches and doodles and endless scribblings about vampire sightings, not to mention another dozen notebooks filled with the facts I could remember that my father had told me over the years. I wish I had all his own detailed notes. I know he had the names—and even photos—of so many vampires. But Blackwatch took everything after he was murdered. A murder Jessop refuses to admit was committed by a vampire.

Clinton Jessop is the Head of Blackwatch. He is also Oliver's boss and, previously, my dad's best friend. They had trained together, worked their way up the ranks together. But, at some point, they'd gone their separate ways. My dad met my mum, at a karaoke night of all places—you'd have to know my dad to realise how absurd that sounds—and they moved to the countryside for a few years, during which time I was born. Jessop stayed in London, continuing his climb to the top of Blackwatch. Then, when I was three, my mum passed away, and we came back to London. Jessop looked out for Dad and me and then just me, after Dad. Generally, he's been a good guy but not about my need for closure.

"There's an agreement in place, Narissa," he told me time and time again, after the murder. "An agreement that's been in place for over two hundred years. No vampire would ever risk breaking the Blood Pact, not after everything they've gained from it."

"They didn't risk breaking it. They fucking obliterated it." (It was probably the first time I'd sworn in his presence, let alone at him.) "I'm telling you: it was a vampire that killed him."

"And I'm telling you: the police say otherwise."

"I saw him, Jessop. I saw the monster that did this."

"You're in shock, that's all. You're putting the knowledge of what your dad did for a job together with a terrible, terrible experience and your brain is making connections where there are none."

So, yeah, fourteen years old, orphaned by a homicidal, supernatural being and no one believed me. I didn't give up, though. I begged Jessop to go to the vampires and find the killer. I begged on my hands and knees more times than any self-respecting person would ever do. I told him that I'd give them a description; it wasn't like the image ever faded from my mind. Seeing those dark, vacuous eyes and pitted skin with the scar above his eyebrow, I knew I'd recognise him in less time than it had taken him to break my dad's neck. But, every time, Jessop said there simply wasn't enough evidence to accuse a vampire. It would create too many problems. I even shoved one of my sketches into his hand, but I don't think he even gave it a second look. He didn't want to know. Two months after the murder, they arrested a man. A drunk, whose hands shook so badly he wouldn't have been capable of snapping a twig, let alone a man's neck. As my mind heads down this particularly unpleasant rabbit hole, my eyes grow heavier and heavier. *Maybe I should move to the bed after all*, is the last thought I have before sleep takes me.

IN THE MORNING, I FEEL JUST AS EXHAUSTED AS THE night before. I'd woken at least half a dozen times. For me, sleep is always fitful. Even without a party going on downstairs, I find it difficult. Sometimes, I wake up in a cold sweat, with images of my father's dead eyes ricocheting around my brain. Other times, I find myself looped in a dream of being lost deep in the woods. I have no idea what wakes me, but I find myself sitting bolt upright, my pulse racing. At least it cuts out the need to set an alarm. At six forty-five, I throw off the covers and switch on the kettle. I've got things to do.

I've only got one lecture this morning: a class on the representation of women in ancient Greek literature, which is probably going to be immensely tragic and depressing, but I'm paying through the nose for this degree and I have no intention of missing any classes. A quick glance at my phone tells me that Joanna has arranged a time for tonight. Eleven o'clock. Later than yesterday, although not really a surprise for someone who's nocturnal.

Unusually for me, shopping is on the cards after uni. Like it or not, I need to look the part this time, and there's no way I can survive that blue coat again. Plus, I need to get it cleaned after the rum soaking it got. Realising I'm going to need some money, I open the bottom drawer of my bedroom tallboy and pull out a tin from beneath the jumble of clothes. When I remove the lid, my heart sinks. Joe's involuntary donation to the Narissa Knight Foundation has not lasted quite as well as I'd hoped, and even with last night's earnings, after paying for fees and rent and other bills, I'm going to be scraping the barrel. Charity shops it is then. That's fine by me.

After a quick shower and a bit of lounging around, I discover there is nothing at all in the flat to eat, so I head out with the plan of stopping at the bakery on the way. Hopefully, I'll be able to keep this thing going with Calin a little while. It would help the money situation considerably.

When I reach the bakery, a woman is sitting on a folded sleeping bag just beside the door. Cardboard boxes are propped up around her and a small, black dog with a handkerchief tied around its neck is nestled in her lap.

"Morning Wendy," I say, offering my first smile of the day as I reach her. "Can I get you anything?"

"Hey, thank you. A cup of tea would be lovely, Naz," she replies, scratching the scruff of the dog's neck. "But don't feel like you have to."

"Nothing to eat?"

"Nah, I'm good. Thank you."

In the café, I order a large cup of tea for Wendy and a bacon sandwich for myself, then quickly change the order to two bacon sandwiches. Wendy might not be hungry at the minute, but I'm sure she'll want something later on. Back outside, I hand her the hot drink and butty and reach down and stroke the dog's neck.

"Have a good day, Jeff," I say, then lift my head. "You too, Wendy."

"You too, love. And you take care. There are some strange folk out there."

"Yes, there are Wendy. Yes, there certainly are."

WHILE I WOULDN'T GO SO FAR AS TO SAY IT HAD BEEN A great day, it was probably above average, with a pretty cool lecture actually. But I am definitely not a fan of this late-night rendezvous lark. It's one thing when you're working in a bar to earn some money, but it's entirely another when you're out in the cold, pounding the pavement in Mayfair, pulling down the hem of your dress and wondering if you're about to walk straight into trouble.

I'm early. Again. And I've got this repetitive swallowing thing going on. There's no reason to suspect this is a trap, is there? Not really, surely. It's not like he can know who I actually am, and it's not like I'm trying to hurt him. Just another of his kind. Still, I'd feel more confident if I was in my normal clothes, rather than the overly clingy, black dress I picked up from the second-hand shop.

It's important to point out that I am not a dress wearer. In fact, until today, I didn't even own one. Nada. Not one. Maybe that seems strange but, given the fact that I was raised by my father, who spent his working hours in the company of century-old, dead people, it's hardly the most unusual thing about me. Anyway, they have always made me irrationally nervous. I can't relax in them. You can't stretch or run or move properly and you never know which part of them is going to let you down. Either they're riding up, or falling too low. So, as I continue to pace and swallow, I'm not sure how much of the stress I'm feeling is down to the fact that I'm about to, once again, willingly offer my body to a member of the undead, under utterly false pretences and how much is to do with this damn dress. Still, the sooner I get this feeding done, the sooner I can get the bloody thing off.

At ten to eleven, after over fifteen minutes of pacing and panicking, I take a deep breath and cross the road to the building. Upstairs, I type the code into the keypad and step inside.

"You didn't have to wait outside for so long."

I nearly wet myself.

"Jeez." I swear I'm panting, as my heart rate attempts to go back to normal. "You're here already?"

"It is my home."

"I know, only last time …" I don't bother with the rest. "Okay. Sure. Yeah."

There's a moment's silence before he speaks again.

"Sorry, I didn't mean to scare you. Can I fetch you a drink? You already know how extensive the range is."

All of this is said in a formal manner that's not the slightest bit inviting. Like he's someone's old-school butler from the 1900s. Maybe he was.

"No, I'm fine."

He's dressed casually again. Jeans and a black T-shirt, taut across his muscular chest—I only mention this for visual accuracy—but there's nothing casual or warm about his demeanour towards me. If anything, it's worse than last night. I'm about to suggest we get straight on with it but remember the whole reason for me being here is to try and find out if he knows the vampire I'm after. That's never going to happen if we don't manage to exchange a sentence that's longer than a few words. Instinctively, my eyes are drawn to a book lying on the coffee table. Maybe that's a way in.

"What are you reading?" I ask with a nod, hoping that it's something I can build a conversation around.

"The Oresteia," he replies. And, just like that, my insides light up. I knew there was a reason I took that module on the representation of women in ancient Greek literature.

Shifting my shoulders back a bit and trying to ignore the restrictions of the dress, I take a few confident steps across to the table.

"It's so hypocritical," I say, in my most scholarly voice. "Don't you think?"

He arches an eyebrow. "What is?"

"The whole thing. How Clytemnestra is treated. She's a queen, seeking revenge for her daughter's murder. That's all."

"And Oreste was just a son, seeking revenge for his father's."

"Which resulted in him killing his own mother. But that's not the hypocritical part. What's wrong is that the gods were fine with it. Fine with him killing Clytemnestra. The fact that they didn't think her daughter's murder was worthy of revenge, despite her being an innocent child, unlike Agamemnon who was a vile, murderous brute, just shows how screwed up the whole thing is."

The smallest of smiles twists on his lips. "You like literature?"

"I like books," I tell him, and there is a flutter in my chest. It's definitely time I look through the rest of the reading list for that course. His amused expression remains for a fraction of a second before it returns to its normal, closed-off look.

"It's late," he says. "Sorry for having to arrange it at this time. I didn't know what time I would be finished with work and I didn't want you to be waiting around here all night."

"Work?" I say, attempting to sound as casual as possible.

"Is not something I wish to discuss in my place of residence," he replies, shutting me down immediately. Worried I'm about to undo the progress made with our shared love of millennia-old Greeks, I move across to the stool at the breakfast bar.

"We should get started," I say. "Do you want to take it from the same arm or the other one?"

"That is entirely up to you."

I take a moment to think it over. Obviously, the cuts are no way healed on my left arm yet, but at least if he feeds close by I'll still need just the one plaster to cover them both up, which will be far easier for Oliver to dismiss, should he notice.

"The same," I say. "And still no scratching."

"I understand."

This time, I'm ready for it. That bolt as fangs pierce skin. The burning sensation as he draws blood out of my veins and into his mouth. Holding my breath, I wait for it to pass. *It'll take just a few seconds*, I remind myself. *It will be over before I can even count to ten. It'll be fine. Easy even.* But, unlike the night before, it doesn't stop straight away. Instead, the pressure increases, and the burning intensifies. I try to focus away from the pain. *Deep breaths.* It's still going. I feel the blood continuing to drain. There's a lightness, starting in my chest, then rising to my head. This is not good. I know it's not. More seconds pass. I should cry out. I want to, but I'm sure he's going to stop. He did before. I open my mouth, but no sound comes out. There's nothing. Just a dizziness. An overwhelming dizziness.

"I … I …" I try to find the words. I try again to make a sound. But I can't. I can't do anything.

Calin

I can still hear the sound of her pulse growing faster and faster, then suddenly fainter. And the taste. The taste was so sweet. Irresistible.

"Calin, are you quite all right?"

"Sorry, Sir?"

"I asked if you were all right. You look quite distant."

"Sorry, Sir. Yes, of course. Please continue."

It takes a second for me to refocus my attention on the group of us around the table. A group which consists of a dozen adults, who couldn't look more mismatched. From the man in the cravat to the woman in the leather jacket, we are, despite outward appearances, a collective. The Vampire Council; select members of the vampire community, tasked with overseeing and governing our kind. Polidori, the Head of the Council, is currently

CHAPTER 10

staring straight at me, a small furrow of concern etched on his brow. Despite my suggestion that he continues, his gaze remains on me.

"A little underfed, perhaps?"

"Perhaps," I agree, although if I were human my cheeks would have turned a flaming red at the outright lie. Underfed is the last thing I am, given that I just drank so much from that poor girl that she passed out. Just thinking about it causes a cold chill to run up my spine.

"Joanna? Joanna?" I knew I'd gone too far the moment her head slumped forwards. Her breathing was laboured, her pulse almost untraceable. For a second I froze, my body utterly paralysed. Then, in an instant, my brain refocused. Darting to the fridge, I grabbed a bottle of water and poured it straight over her head.

"Shit. How?" Talking to myself, I lifted her, now dripping wet, over to the bed. It's been the best part of a century since I've drained a person to death and I promised myself that I would never do it again. Maybe it was the lack of venom that made her blood so moreish. Or the fact that I had been so reticent to feed properly the day before. Restraint with live donors can be difficult at the best of times but particularly when you're out of practice.

"Please, please just wake up."

I could hear her heart beat start to steady and, deep down, I knew that she would be fine, but those few minutes waiting lasted longer than the whole previous decade. To kill a human, accident or not, would go against the Blood Pact. Against everything we'd fought to protect.

A cough was her first reaction. Then a splutter.

"Dad," she whispered, quietly.

Gasping with relief, I dropped down onto the bed next to her and felt the warmth returning to her skin.

"Thank God," I said.

Only then did I think of the time. The Council gathering —this gathering—was due to start in less than an hour and excuses are not easily accepted. Perhaps it would be best, I considered, if I left before she woke fully. She was already blinking herself back to consciousness. No doubt she would be racing off to Blackwatch, to inform them of my indiscretion. If it got to Jessop, it would get to Polidori too. He had forgiven me for far worse in the past but not when I was a member of the Council. In a split-second decision, I scribbled on a piece of paper and grabbed an envelope from the desk drawer. A second later, as she rolled over and blinked her eyes open, I was gone.

"I'll go." The Council is silent. All eyes on Polidori. Across the table, Damien Styx, another member —quite possibly my least favourite—is sitting shoulders back, arms folded. My brief reminiscence has, once again, left me unsure as to what has been said and therefore what he has just volunteered himself for. "It shouldn't take long to sort out," he says.

"No, no." Polidori shakes his head. "You have work to be getting on with here. Calin, I would like you to go up there instead. See if you can't get this matter sorted as quickly as possible."

Racking my brains, I try to deduce what it is he's talking about, but I'm not fast enough. Styx reads the confusion in my face in a moment and sneers in response.

"Humans have been killed up by the Scottish border."

"A rogue?"

"It would appear that way," says Polidori, taking back control of the conversation. "The matter shouldn't take more than a few days to clear up. Discreetly of course. You can leave tonight, I assume."

There's no question mark at the end of his words and rightly so. As the Head of the Council, Polidori doesn't need to ask. He tells. Still, I hesitate. Killing rogue vampires is not something I enjoy. Killing anything is not something I like to do. Besides, I was hoping to see the girl again. Not to feed, just to apologise. Clear the air. Then again, there is a fair chance that she won't be responding to my messages any time soon.

"Of course, Sir," I say, offering the only response I can. "I'll leave immediately."

"Very good. Well, that is all we have to discuss for now. I'll bid you all good day."

As the rest of the Council rise to leave, I follow suit although I am barely out of my seat when I hear my name called yet again.

"Calin, a word, if I may."

"Of course."

While the others filter out, I remain standing. Finally, when Polidori and I are the only two left, he moves from his seat to close the door.

"Are you sure you're quite all right? You don't seem like yourself tonight."

"Honestly, Sir, I'm absolutely fine. But thank you again for your concern."

"Don't be silly. I think of you as a son, you know

that." He offers me a smile that is far more genuine than any I had seen around the table that night. While many vampires are happy with a solitary life, Polidori is not one of those. He saved my life by changing me, a hundred years back now, and has been, as he said, a father figure to me ever since. Teaching me to navigate this world. Teaching me that I still have a place in it. When the Vampire Council was set up, he was the perfect choice to spearhead it: cautious, but optimistic. A human-lover to the core. And someone who has seamlessly blended into their world for years.

"I do."

With a quick nod of his head, he is back to his original point. "This business going on in Scotland. Please tread as lightly as you can. There are other parties in the area who may be concerned by yet more of our presence."

"You mean Blackwatch?"

"No. Just find the rogue vampire, eliminate it and come back."

"Yes, Sir."

"Excellent. Thank you. Well, I should let you go. No doubt you have packing to do. Report straight to me on your return."

"Of course."

Having been dismissed, I open the large, oak door into the corridor and I'm now considering not only if leaving the girl had been the right choice but also wondering what I am going to have to deal with when I arrive in Scotland. Although there is little time to dwell on this as, barely out of the room, I get ambushed from the side.

CHAPTER 10

"Sheridan." My muscles stiffen. Only one person calls me by my surname, and he's the one person on the Council I try to avoid more than any other.

"Styx," I respond and continue walking, knowing that he's going to follow and knowing it's just easier to let him say whatever it is he's going to say. He's your classic playground bully, only he's two hundred and fifty years old and has a set of top canines that can punch holes in leather. If the rumours are to be believed, when the Blood Bank is open, he helps himself to three Blackwatch live donors a night and all at the Council's expense. In short, he's vile.

"You seemed very distracted in there," he says, falling into step beside me, his face contorted into its standard sneer. "The thought of having to go and do some actual work get you all worried? Did Daddy want to check that you were feeling okay? Underfed? Like hell." He leans over at me and sniffs deeply. "I can smell human all over you. Is that the distraction?"

Every word that comes out of his mouth makes me shudder. He's not the only one like it, of course—a vampire that, deep down, believes they're better than humans. I wouldn't be surprised if he's still got his lower fangs, kept in a jar somewhere, ready to fondle, as he reminisces about the good-old days, when he was free to drain whoever he wanted. And yet, Polidori trusts him, and when you've been around as long as he has, you become a pretty good judge of character. There must be something I'm missing. That said, I'm not going to hang around with him long enough to find out what that might be.

"And you know, if you can't remember how to put down a stray," he says, "maybe I can help you out?"

He has left himself wide open. I stop and look him straight in the eye.

"Are you offering to let me practice on you? Because I'd happily take you up on that. I'll go and grab a stake right now."

His sneer drops by just a fraction, and I manage to keep my feeling of satisfaction to myself, as I start heading for the front door again.

"I'll see you at the next Council gathering, Styx," I say, pulling an umbrella from the stand. I'm pretty sure it always rains in Scotland.

11

Narissa

Well, this is shit.
At this point, it's fair to say my plan to befriend the vampire and get him to lead me to my dad's killer has gone south pretty fast. On the plus side, if vampires do ever become common knowledge, I've now got a great story to tell the grandkids. *Once, children, a vampire nearly killed me by drinking almost all my blood and, afterwards, he put me to bed in his beautiful, Egyptian-cotton sheets, before he pissed off into the night.*

"Calin?" I call. There is no response.

My head is throbbing and, for an instant, I think that the liquid I can feel dripping from my hair is blood. I gingerly open my eyes and spy the empty, mineral-water bottle on the bedside table.

"Are you serious?" I ask. Even those few words cause

my head to spin. Slowly, I push myself up onto my elbows. How long have I been out? Looking around for a clock makes my head swim again and immediately forces me to close my eyes. I don't think it has been that long. It doesn't feel like that long. Then again, I've never fainted before. (Honestly. Not once. Is that weird?) After a few deep breaths, I open my eyes again, only to notice an envelope with "Joanna" scrawled on it. I don't have to open it to know what's inside, but I do anyway.

"You have to be kidding me."

Flicking through the envelope only makes me madder. I'm pissed off. A note—and by note, I mean the word "sorry", written in crazily curly writing that looks like it belongs in some calligraphy workbook—and a wad of cash. I've been treated better by one-night stands that left after the job was done and stole the last slice of pizza on the way out. Surely, he should have at least stayed to check I wasn't dead, even if he did lay me down on the most comfortable bed in the world.

My eyes go to the wound on my arm. It's far darker than the previous one. The deep, red, puncture marks are still dripping. Maybe I'll smear some blood on his perfect bedding. That'll serve him right. Although I quickly change my mind. Now that I'm starting to come to my senses, the reality of my situation starts to sink in. And it's not a great feeling. For a while, I sit in absolute silence. Sounds filter in from outside, distant and detached.

"What the hell are you doing, Naz?" I say to myself, once again looking at my arm. "Christ, what is wrong with you?"

A lump catches in the back of my throat and I can feel tears pooling in the corners of my eyes, but I refuse to let them fall. Not here. Not in the home of one of these monsters. I push myself off the bed. I'm a little wobbly on my feet. The dizziness passes, but a sudden heat is overwhelming me, and sweat is starting to run down the back of my neck. I could have got myself killed. That could have been it. How fucking stupid can you get? Picking up the envelope and my phone, I swipe for an Uber and get out of there as fast as I can, not even bothering to check if the door closes behind me.

I've set the car to take me straight to the one place I know I'll be safe. Obviously, there is zero chance of me telling Oliver why I'm turning up at gone midnight, yet again, or why I'm trembling quite so much.

Fortunately, he is not in interrogation mode tonight.

"You don't look good," he says, rubbing his eyes and squinting at me through a layer of sleep. "Is everything all right?"

I nod, almost pushing past him to get into the flat. I know the whole thing about vampires having to be invited in is bullshit, so I feel a damn-sight safer having a bolted door behind me and a homeowner with a gun nearby, however ridiculous that might sound.

"Just a touch of flu," I lie, fetching myself a large glass of water and downing it in one. "Are you okay if I sleep on the sofa? I just didn't want to be on my own, you know, in case the fever gets worse or anything."

For a moment, he stands there and watches me. The sleepiness of only moments ago has gone and, in its place, is a different expression. One I don't want to examine too closely. I wait, trying to hide the tremble in my hand, as I clutch the glass.

"You should take the bed," he says, eventually. "Otherwise, I'll wake you in the morning when I go to work."

"I'll be fine on the sofa," I assure him, but he changes the bedding anyway. When it's finally ready, he pulls back the quilt for me, then places a fresh glass of water on the bedside table.

"You didn't have to do this," I say, my body moving involuntarily towards the bed. There's no way I'm going to put up any more of a fight, and the sheets may not be Egyptian cotton or whatever, but the moment my head hits the pillow, I swear it's the most comfortable bed I've ever been in. With a deep sigh, I close my eyes and, still fully clothed, pull the quilt over me.

"Naz?" I half listen as Oliver's voice floats around me. "Is there something you want to talk about?"

"Uh-uh,"

I sense him still lingering there, hovering, watching.

"You know you can tell me anything, right? You know I won't judge you."

A niggle of guilt is worming its way into my sleepy brain. I keep my eyes closed and pray it doesn't show.

"I know," I say, with a fake yawn.

Another pause follows and, for a second, I think he's going to say something else. His breath is held I realise but, there again, so is mine. I wonder if he can tell. But just as I think he's about to speak, there's the creaking of floorboards and the closing of the bedroom door. I'm alone. And then, for the first time in more years than I can remember, I let myself cry.

12

It's pretty pathetic, but for the past three days I haven't left Oliver's flat. I don't know why. It's really tough to explain. I knew vampires existed. I've always known. I grew up with stories about them, the same way normal people grow up with stories about farm animals and the solar system. Hell, I watched one kill my father. But they had always seemed somehow detached, like they existed on another plane. Like I was somehow safe from them. Even after the first donor session, I still felt like that. Not surprising really—I've given worse hickies than that first bite. I guess I thought that would be it. Now I know it's not, and it feels like the world has spun just a little bit more off its axis. Fortunately, I've had company for the last day and a half.

"Are you dating someone?"

"What?"

"Or thinking about dating someone? Because I swear you haven't managed thirty seconds in this last hour without looking at your phone. So, I figure you've got to be dating someone. Or at least want to be. Is that why you're here? Trying to get Oliver into bed, as a distraction from whoever it is you're pining over?"

"You have a one-track mind. And no, I'm not. Besides, who uses the word *pining* anymore?"

"Two," Rey replies, completely unhelpfully.

"Sorry? What?"

"Two. I have a two-track mind. Sex and magic. Don't forget about the magic."

"Fine, you have a two-track mind."

"I'd say that's probably about right."

I don't know what I'm expecting Calin to say or what I even want him to say, for that matter. He's a vampire, for crying out loud. The rational part of me knows this. But, surely, common courtesy dictates he sends some kind of an apology text, at the very least, via Joanna, of course. Sighing, I continue to stare at my phone.

I guess what upsets me is that fact that I read him so wrongly. For some reason, I got the impression he was the Blackwatch's poster boy for vampirism. A pillar of integrity. One for whom human-vampire relationships mattered. I mean, we talked about literature. Greek literature. Albeit very briefly. But still … now I feel like I've been ghosted by a dead guy. Which would probably be funny in a different situation.

"Come on, then. Don't keep it to yourself. Who is this mystery person?"

"Honestly, there's no one."

"Well, something's going on. I don't think I've ever seen you like this before. You know you can tell me anything, right?"

The exact same words that Oliver had said to me,

when I first turned up here a few nights ago. For a split second, I consider telling her. Not just about Calin but everything. I could tell her how I can't get close to anyone because the thought of losing them is enough to rip open a thousand tiny cuts that have never had a chance to heal. Or that, every day, I'm so lonely that I'm terrified that if I stop, even for a minute, I might never get moving again. But she'd say she knows all that. So, I could tell her there are other things she doesn't know. Like, when she left a year ago, when she was forced out of my life, I drank my way through the best part of a week. That lying to people is the only way I feel I can keep them safe. That, even though Calin nearly killing me was one of the most horrific experiences of my life, I'm also glad he did. Because him messing up like that might just be the *in* I've been desperate for. Because the only value I place on my life is finding out who took my dad's.

"Naz?" She looks at me expectantly and I feel the words on the tip of my tongue. If I do tell her, then what? She's got her own mission, without mine getting in the way. And, even though she's split from Blackwatch, the last thing I want to do is jeopardise her friendship with Oliver. I know where I stand now. I know that I'm going to find Dad's killer or die trying. That's not something I can put on her. With a shake of my head, I put my phone down on the coffee table.

"It's a job, if you must know," I say, pushing aside the other thoughts and finding I can come up with a lie incredibly easily.

"That's cool. What kind of job?"

"Just some graduate scheme. I probably don't have a chance."

Am I a bad person? Surely only bad people lie as easily as I do. Then again, I remind myself, I'm lying to keep her safe. I am already on Blackwatch's radar. The last thing Rey needs is to be associated with me.

"But it's cool that you applied."

"Yeah, maybe." I just want to end the lie as soon as possible.

Ready to twist the conversation back to her and talk of grimoires, I open my mouth to speak, when my phone buzzes loudly on the table. The pair of us jump, although I only offer it a half glance. Oliver has texted at least five times a day since I arrived, asking if I want him to pick up some Lemsip or Ibuprofen or whatever and, even when I say no, he comes back with them anyway. But, this time, the phone is ringing and it's not Oliver's name on the screen.

"Is that it?" she asks. "Is that the job?"

"Do you mind if I just take this in private for a second?"

Private isn't really something Rey and I do but, at the same time, respect is. Without me needing to ask a second time, she's on her feet.

"No worries, you go for it. I was just gonna go down to the shops anyway. We're out of crisps and chocolate. You need anything?"

I shake my head as I pick up the phone. It's still ringing, and I'm sure they're going to hang up soon, but I wait until she is out the door before I finally answer.

"Joanna," I say, my voice cracking. "Have you heard from him?"

Whether it's my imagination or not, it feels like her

voice takes an age to come down the line. When it does, she sounds even more on edge than before.

"He left me a voice message just now. I nearly picked up. He nearly heard my voice."

So that explains the nervousness.

"It's fine. You didn't. What did he say? What was the message?"

There's a hiss down the line, as she sucks in a breath. "He said he's sorry. And that he wants to see you tonight. He's really sorry about something by the sounds of it. He's been away, apparently. He said you could meet in public, though, if you felt safer. Look Narissa, I know you're—"

"Tell him yes."

"Pardon?"

"Tell him yes. I'll meet him."

A short pause follows, before she speaks again. "Look, I feel like I should have more of an idea what's going on here. The guy sounded really guilty. And what did he mean *safer?* What exactly is he apologising for?"

I'm not even listening properly at this point. "I'll send you the name of a bar," I say, not even sure if she's still talking or not. "And tell him he'll be the one paying."

13

With Rey still at the shops, I stuff my few belongings into a carrier bag and head for the door. As bad luck would have it, the minute I reach for the handle, the door opens.

"You're going out?" Oliver asks, coming in. "Are you feeling better? You know I don't mind you sticking around a bit longer, if you want."

He's so sweet it makes my chest ache for lying to him. Still, it's for a greater good.

"Thanks," I say, genuinely meaning it. "But I've already imposed on you way too long. I need to get back to lectures. Besides, you've already got Rey here."

"Where is she?" Oliver casts a quick glance over my shoulder. "I thought she'd be in."

"She went out to fetch a few things. She won't be long."

"In that case I'm going to jump in the shower before she comes back and steals all the hot water." He offers me a fleeting grin, before the seriousness returns. "You know

I mean it. You can stay as long as you need. Whenever you need."

"I know." Reaching up on tiptoes, I plant a kiss on his cheek. "I'll text you later."

Then I slip past him and leave without looking back.

After so many nights at Oliver's place, my flat feels like a cold, dark dump. Which it is, but I'm not going to be here for long. After a quick deliberation over what to wear, I opt for a long-sleeved, polo neck and jeans, with a hoodie over the top. I'm not letting a scrap of skin show. Given the dress I wore before, it's not exactly a subtle hint as to how I'm feeling. Then it's straight back out. Time to meet the vampire. Again.

I suggested a bar near the Apollo Victoria Theatre, not far from my old flat. It's easy to get to on the tube and the theatre environment ensures a constant stream of people. Bright lights, busy crowds and familiar territory; I'm not taking any chances tonight.

I arrive twenty minutes before our arranged time, while it is still light, so I can get the lie of the land before I meet him. However, I haven't even got my hands on my rum and coke when Calin appears beside me. I do my best to hide my surprise.

"Thank you." They are the first words out of his mouth, as he pulls out a stool and sits down at the bar next to me. "Thank you for meeting me. I'm sure you understand my need to apologise. I'm so sorry about what happened."

With a stylish grey flat cap pulled low over his eyes

and a scarf around his neck, it's a far cry from the tight T-shirts he's worn before. Dad was right then; vampires can go out in daylight. They just prefer not to.

"What for?" I ask, as the barman passes me my drink which I take without even looking. "For nearly killing me? For drenching me with water? Or for leaving a scrawled message with a wad of cash, instead of waiting around to see if I was actually okay."

"I knew you were okay," he says, with a mixture of earnestness and defensiveness. "I would never have left otherwise."

"Really? And what would you have done if I hadn't been okay? Called up Blackwatch and explained your situation?"

I watch his Adam's apple bob up and down. Another moment ticks by before he speaks again.

"I did not behave appropriately, on any level," he says, eventually. "And I am sorry. Sincerely so."

A polite throat clearing alerts us to the barman who is now staring at Calin.

"Can I get you a drink?" he asks.

"I'll take a small scotch please. Whatever you have is fine."

With a nod, the barman disappears, leaving an awkward silence between us.

"Why did you meet me?" Calin asks eventually, looking me dead in the eye, and all the hairs on my neck stand on end. It takes every bit of willpower not to look away.

"So you could apologise. Why else?"

"No, that's not it."

"It's not?" I peer down my nose at him, giving him

CHAPTER 13

my most decidedly unimpressed look. "Then, please, enlighten me as to what my intentions are, as you apparently know me better than I know myself."

He continues to stare, unblinking. Not cold, but there's iron in his resolve. Whether it's my imagination or not, it feels like everyone in the bar has suddenly fallen silent.

"I don't. I don't know anything about you," he says, almost in a whisper. "I don't know why you didn't contact Blackwatch the minute you woke. I don't know why you barely flinched when you first saw what I was. I don't know you, Joanna, but I want to. So, tell me, what is it you want?"

What *do* I want? I want revenge. That's it, plain and simple. And maybe if I tell him, he'll help me get it. Then again, maybe he won't. So, instead, I stick to the original script.

"I want to get to know you better," I say.

It's not meant to sound seductive, and I don't think it does, but still his eyes remain on me, as if searching all the way deep inside, as they refuse to soften. Then, slowly, he offers a single, slight nod.

"Okay," he says. "What does that mean?"

It's actually a good question. What I mean is, I want to learn about all of your acquaintances, in the hope that one of them is the one I'm looking for, so that I can slit his throat and put a stake through his heart. Once again, I am forced to rethink my phrasing.

"I just want to learn about what you are. About your kind. What you can do? How many of you there are?"

His lips twist. "That's not the way things work. This is a business arrangement. We aren't going to become friends or anything else, for that matter. That's how Blackwatch wants it."

"Then maybe we need to leave Blackwatch out of this."

I take a pen out of my bag, pull the napkin out from under my glass and scribble down my actual phone number on it.

"I've got a new number," I say, before standing up and slinging my bag over my shoulder. I know he's going to call.

"What about your drink?" he asks.

I pick up the glass and down it in one, then turn and leave.

Outside the bar, I don't look back as I walk away. After twenty yards or so, I duck down a side street, then take a right down an even-narrower alleyway. It worked, I'm certain of it. He's already gone against Blackwatch, meeting me like this. I wouldn't be surprised if he's messaged me before I even get home.

I'm already so consumed by my phone, waiting for it to ping, that I don't see the two figures appear dead ahead of me. Nor do I sense the one coming up behind me. Not until I hear a voice that causes fear to twist like a knife in my gut.

"Narissa Knight. Well, well, as I live and breathe. I've been looking everywhere for you."

14

My first instinct is to run. His goons are blocking the way ahead but, while they're big, I know from seeing the way they handle punters at the bar, that they're not exactly fast. Maybe if it was just one of them, I could get clear. But two? I'm not so sure. Turning around, I'm face-to-face with Joe himself. At first glance, Joe Trench is not the sort of man you'd be intimidated by: just five feet two, receding hairline and a paunch that implies he hasn't seen a vegetable or a gym in years, if ever. But that would be because you don't know him. I've seen what he can do. I've seen him nail a man's hand to the bar for spilling his drink, then walk away and fetch himself another pint, like he's just been doing some DIY. So, while I could try to run by him, I wouldn't put it past him to put a bullet in my leg, or somewhere else. Particularly likely as I'm fairly certain that bulge in his pocket isn't because he's pleased to see me.

Maybe I should scream. Maybe drawing attention to myself will be the only way out of this. I'm still thinking through what my next move should be, when he starts speaking again.

"I have to admit, I do enjoy a little bit of irony," he says, walking slowly towards me and tapping his hand on his thigh in a way that makes my blood run cold. The tapping is a nervous twitch he's got. Something he does before he really lets rip. I've seen it dozens of times before, only this is the first time I've ever been on the receiving end.

"Seeing you, like this, at this moment in time. You see, I was just thinking about you. Thinking what I should do to someone who knowingly took advantage of my generosity. Who knowingly made a fool out of me. What could I do that would be fair compensation for the humiliation that you heaped on me? That's what I was thinking. And, as that exact thought was crossing my mind, do you know what happened?"

There's a pause but I'm pretty sure it's a rhetorical question, so I decide it's probably best to keep my mouth shut.

"I see you, sitting in a bar, bold as brass. And I thought, 'Oh fate has been kind to me tonight'. Don't you agree Narissa? Good things always come to those who wait. Actually, I think I'm rather glad about the cat-and-mouse games you've been playing. Because it's gonna be all the more fun to beat the crap out of you."

The sensible part of me knows I need to keep my mouth shut. The rest of me struggles with this advice.

"Just to be clear here, which part of that was irony? You could definitely say that it was a coincidence, serendipitous even, but I'm not sure you fully grasp the concept of irony."

His mouth twists. "You little bitch."

As Joe gets angrier, my head is whirring. I need to think of a plan, and quickly. I have to keep him talking, while I come up with something. Taking a step forwards, I offer him the best and most disarming smile I can manage, given the situation.

"Hey, look, there's no need to be like that. In fact, I'm glad I've run into you. I've been meaning to come by the bar for the last week now."

He sneers. "Like hell you have."

"No, honestly. You know I was doing some maths and, when I looked at the numbers, I realised I should have taken at least another seven hundred to make us even on what you owe me."

His cheeks turn an unnatural shade of puce.

"Oh, Narissa, am I ever gonna make you pay?"

"As opposed to you *actually* paying me, which is what you should have done to stop us getting into this mess in the first place?"

"You think you're so smart, don't you?"

Actually, at this precise moment, no, I don't. I think I'm an idiot. The idea was to keep him talking, while I thought of a plan. Instead, all that's happening is he's getting more and more angry at me. This happens when I get stressed. My brain and mouth fully disconnect. I need to back up. Sound more sincere. I need to get out of the damn alley for starters.

"How about this then?"

Sensing movement behind me, I take a step towards him again, trying to hide the fact that I'm absolutely bricking it.

"You let me go; no hard feelings. I won't draw attention to any authorities about the tax violations, the underage workers, the below-minimum wage paid, the lack of health and safety in the restaurant. And we call it quits. Sound like a good deal?"

"How about I make sure you can't ever talk to any authorities, or anyone else, ever again? Sounds like a better deal to me."

I'm out of time, and I know it. And, still, there's nobody within shouting distance. The only option I am left with is to do what I probably should have done at the very beginning. Run and scream for help.

"Help!" I yell, as I make a split-second decision to run in Joe's direction. I'm hoping I can barge past him but, in my panic, I hadn't noticed how much closer Tweedledum and Dee have got. I've barely made it three feet, when one of them grabs me by the shoulder.

"No, she's mine."

Joe pushes him away, only to slam his fist straight into my stomach. I topple backwards, gasping and crashing onto the pavement with barely time to close my eyes before his boot comes at me. The first kick is straight to the stomach again. In the split second as he pulls his leg back to strike once more, I roll myself into the foetal position, grabbing my knees and turning my face away. The next strike is to my ribs. As a bone cracks, a scream escapes me into the night. My eyes are still clenched shut and I can taste blood in my mouth. *Let it end soon*, is what I'm thinking. *Just let it be swift.* There's no way out of this now. He'll see the job through. I'm certain of it. My whole body is braced for the next kick. My throat tightens, as I'm struggling to pull in another breath of air. *Please*, I think. *Just do it. Just get it over with.* Another moment passes. What the hell is he playing at? Who stops half way through beating someone up? That's when I hear the yelp of pain.

Hesitantly opening my eyes, I lift my head just enough to see what's going on. Joe is no longer standing over me. In fact, none of them are. The two goons are lying flat on their backs. Grimacing against the pain, I push myself to my knees. That's when I see them. Joe, white as a ghost, pinned to the wall, feet dangling in the air, a pale hand clasped around his throat.

"Calin," I gasp.

15

His two henchmen are starting to stir, groaning. I am relieved they're not dead, although I'm not sure I'd have shed that many tears if they had been. Besides, I don't have much time to dwell on the matter. On the other side of the alley, Joe's eyes are bulging from their sockets.

"I, I …"

"You won't ever go near her again," Calin hisses, as he moves in closer until his nose is almost touching Joe's. "Do you understand me? You will never lay a finger on her again."

A shallow, unintelligible spluttering comes from Joe's mouth.

"Is that a yes? I can't hear you properly." Calin's voice is unlike anything I've ever heard before. So clear, so cold, it freezes the air around him. He loosens his grip by just a fraction and Joe coughs a few more incomprehensible words, before he's able to speak clearly.

"Fu … fuck you," he manages to spit.

Then he pulls his head back and brings it down hard into Calin's face. In my mind, I play out what happens next. I see the sharp twist of Joe's head, hear the sound of his vertebrae snapping, before his lifeless body finally slides down to the tarmac. But Calin doesn't even flinch. Instead, he lowers him to the ground.

"I'll give you one more chance to make the right choice," he offers, as he turns his back on the thug and takes a step away from him.

Before I can warn him, Joe reaches inside his pocket and pulls out a gun.

"How about *I* give *you* one more chance to make the right choice?" he sneers.

"I'll take that as a *no* then," says Calin, turning back around.

"Take it however—"

His words are cut short, as Calin snatches the gun and drives the barrel into Joe's thigh with such a force, the crunching sound reverberates around the alley. He falls to the ground, clutching his leg and sobbing. By contrast, Calin straightens himself up and fixes his clothes.

"Now to be clear," he says. "You are nothing to me. This girl," he points to me, "she is under my protection. You so much as look in her direction, and I will rip those eyeballs straight from their sockets. I will hunt you down and make you feel pain the likes of which you can't even imagine. Do you understand now?"

Still whimpering, Joe nods in agreement. Calin turns his head to the two goons, who are now standing, slack jawed, and gestures to their boss. They rush in and pull him to his feet and all three of them stumble and limp away, throwing furtive glances over their shoulders the whole way. I go to stand myself, but I have barely shifted position, when he is there, beside me. Reaching down a hand.

"So, *Narissa?*"

"Actually I prefer Naz," I say with a weak smile.

"We need to get you to hospital."

"No, I'll be fine. I'll be fine."

Blood trickles down my chin. From the way my mouth is stinging, I'd guess I've got a pretty hefty split lip. Not to mention the various cracked ribs I can feel grinding beneath my skin with every breath I take. Broken ribs are nasty, yes, but generally they heal.

"There might be internal bleeding. We need to get you checked out. Here, let me stop the pain a bit."

Even before I see the nail, I know exactly what he's going to do. Instinctively, I push myself away from him, ignoring the pain that shoots up my side as I do so.

"No, not that freaking nail!" I yell at him, shaking my head and resting my hands on my knees, to stop myself from falling. "Human drugs, good. Weird, vampire venom, bad."

"It'll stop it hurting," he tries again.

"No. No. You can take me to the hospital, though."

"Okay. We'll move fast. I'll carry you." I feel one arm hook around my back and the other behind my knees as he effortlessly lifts me up. I close my eyes and wait for him to start moving. The pain in my ribs and chest is now joined by one in my ankle. I must have twisted it, when Joe knocked me over. While I'm not going to risk freaky vampire venom for anything, I definitely think a shot of morphine might be on the cards at the hospital. Only we're not moving.

"Calin?" I say, opening my eyes. I see his are fixed ahead and I turn painfully to find what he's looking at.

My gaze falls on the barrel of yet another gun. This one is different though, not a regular handgun. It's part of a modified Glock 9mm, with a gas compressor firing mechanism, and the clip almost certainly contains ironwood bullets. How do I know all this? Because it's Blackwatch issue and my father had one just like it.

"Oliver?"

16

"Of all the stupid things."

Oliver, rather than Calin, is the one who has accompanied me to the hospital and, after several hours of waiting, I'm told I have four cracked ribs, a sprained ankle, and a large amount of bruising. As I suspected, there's nothing that can be done about any of that, although I'm given a substantial bottle of painkillers to get me through the next couple of days.

While Oliver remains by my side in A&E, he's not what you'd call supportive. Mostly he offers endless glowers and glares, tuts and occasionally swear words, less than subtly directed at me. To give him his due, he manages to keep his temper in check around the doctors and nurses although, the moment I discharge myself and limp my way to his car, he lets it all rip.

"What the hell were you thinking, Narissa?" he demands, using my full name as he slams his jeep door shut. "How did you ever think this was a good idea?"

"Which idea is the bad one?" I say sleepily. I'm not

trying to be facetious. I'm trying to ask a genuine question, but the drugs are making it difficult.

Rather than rewarding my efforts, he turns the key in the ignition and huffs loudly.

"You're right. Because you have so many bad ideas, Naz. Seriously. It's like you have a death wish. I can't believe you've been blood donoring."

Did I tell him that I wonder? I know that was something I really didn't want him to know, so it seems strange that I'd let it slip, even with the painkillers. I look down at my hands and, a second later, join the dots. Literally.

"You saw the marks on my arm."

"Yes, Narissa, I saw the *bite* marks on your arm. How? How did you even manage that? Blackwatch monitors all blood donors. Especially to someone like Calin Sheridan."

"You left one of the printouts on your desk," I reply, my mouth letting the truth slip out before my brain can stop it. "I found the date and time and got there first. Said I'd split the cash with her. Joanna, that's the girl's name. She's quite nice. You'd like her."

Once again, the painkillers have let me down and I sense his anger before I hear it, which I do, very loud, as he slams his fist down on the horn on the steering wheel, sending a blast out into the road.

"Shit, Narissa, this just gets worse and worse. Do you not see how many ways this could have gone wrong? Blackwatch controls donors for a reason. To keep them safe. Not to mention the fact that I will lose my job if Jessop finds out. You see that, right? You realise that this could cost me my career?"

"But Calin won't say anything. He nearly killed me

and didn't say anything. He just gave me extra money …" Crap. I've done it again. I rapidly try to back track. "Forget I said that, okay? I shouldn't have told you that. Besides, I'm fine. See? All fine."

"For crying out loud." His fist comes down again and, this time, the driver in front of us turns in anger and flips us the finger. "Why? Why are you so obsessed?"

Even all the painkillers in the world couldn't stop me reacting to that one. My eyes ping open as I turn and face him.

"Why do you think? It was one of them. One of them killed him. If I can just get close to him—"

"No, Naz. Just no. You're going to wind up dead, over an obsession that is misplaced. A vampire did *not* kill your father. Jessop has told you this. I have told you this."

"They're hiding things. Even if Jessop doesn't know it, one of them does. The vampires up the top, they know something."

"No. Nothing's hidden, Naz. The Blood Pact works. It's worked for two hundred years. Your father was not killed by a vampire, but by a sick, sick man. It was a terrible accident. That's all. A really horrendous accident."

"Why won't you—"

"I've had enough, Naz! You need to get over this."

Silence fills the car. A silence which I have no intention of breaking. *Get over it?* Does he honestly believe that it's that straightforward? Part of me wants to scream at him. *I'd like a normal life!* I want to say. *I'd like to be able to go to the pub with my friends and have my only worries be what I'm going to wear for a job interview, or why it's been four days since a guy I dated last messaged. I'd like to be ignorant, like the majority of the seven billion people on the planet, and think that vampires are from the imagination of writers and storytellers. Men in dark capes that turn into bats, inhabiting only the nightmares of children.* But I'm not. I know the truth. And I also know the Blood Pact doesn't work. For at least one vampire out there.

"Where are you living now?" he asks, quietly, breaking my stream of thought.

"Sorry?"

"Your address. Where do you live now? I need to know, so I can drop you home."

"Are we not going back to yours?"

Another second of silence follows.

"I'm sorry, Naz, I can't do this. I need some time to clear my head. Decide what I'm supposed to do."

A substantial lump has lodged itself in my throat. What did I think, that he'd find out the truth and be just fine with it? No, of course I didn't. But had I considered that in this state, bloodied and beaten up, he would just dump me on my own? Not for a second. A deep pain, that has nothing to do with my damaged ribs, burns in my chest.

"Tower Hamlets," I say, in a voice far quieter than normal. "My flat is over in Tower Hamlets."

17

He doesn't offer to walk me to the door, or even ask if I am all right to get up to the flat on my own. Instead, he parks the car where I say, in front of a large grey tower block and I hobble off alone. He's watching me though. I can still see his car through the glass front door, as I step into the lift. This whole thing would be infinitely easier if we'd had serious disagreements before. You know, if we were the type of friends who regularly argued but then made it up again with dramatic gestures and copious amounts of alcohol. But we're not. We've never had any type of falling out. There's been an unspoken agreement between us that nothing would be big enough to wreck our friendship—which is also, I guess, why we've never been anything more than just friends. We've always known we'd be there for each other. The thing is, Oliver has never really needed me the way I've often needed him. And now I have done the one thing that could truly push him away for good.

CHAPTER 17

Stepping into the flat is like stepping into an icebox, and it's not until I limp my way to the bedroom that I realise I've left one of the windows open.

After closing the offending window and switching on the heating, I curl up under a blanket on the sofa and consider what the hell I'm doing with my life.

Thanks to Calin, I've probably got enough money to see me straight for a couple of months, but that's it. No job, no donor money. And I've missed the last couple of days of lectures, too. So much for the brilliant first-class degree I was planning on getting. A bitter laugh escapes my lips, which leads to a painful coughing fit.

The exchange in the side street, before Oliver whisked me off to hospital, had been brief but long enough for me to realise that he and Calin most definitely know each other. There's no chance of me getting close to him and finding my vampire now. And there's no chance of me finding another vampire either. If Oliver ever allows me back into his flat again, he'll most likely have the door to his office padlocked.

After popping another two painkillers, I lay my head back down on the cushions and close my eyes. Maybe it'll all seem better in the morning.

Given that I forgot to draw the curtains, the morning light is streaming through the window, causing me to squint as I open my eyes. By my side, the bottle of painkillers is still open. Maybe I should just take one of them at a time in future. Clearly, they have the ability to seriously knock you out. That said, I reach for the bottle again, hoping to lessen the pounding in my head. It's only when my eyes are fully open, that I realise the pounding is coming from the front door, not my temples.

"Naz? Naz? Are you in there? Open up. Oliver told me what happened. Are you okay?"

That's a lot to deal with, particularly when you've only just woken up, have no idea what time of day it is, and the person speaking to you isn't even in the room. Still, I know she's not going to stop. Biting down against the pain, I push myself upright and stumble over to the front door.

"Holy shit, Naz."

I haven't looked at myself in a mirror since I got home, but judging from the horror on Rey's face, I'd say it's not good.

"Did Oliver send you?" I ask, stepping back slowly to make way for her.

"Of course he did." She's carrying a plastic bag, which she dumps just inside the door before wrapping her arms around me and giving me a careful hug. Even so, her arms cause a shooting pain in my left side. I suck it down the best I can and hope she doesn't see.

"How is he?" I ask, hobbling back to the sofa. "Still mad?"

"Yes. Very definitely still mad. But it's early days. You'll have to give him time. He'll come around."

"You think he'll tell Jessop?"

She shakes her head. "No. It's not his job he's worried about, it's you. That's what we're all worried about. Why didn't you ask us for help?"

Tears are starting to burn in my eyes, and I can't see any point in keeping them hidden.

"I have asked. I spent years asking Oliver and Jessop for help, but they refuse to believe me."

"It's obvious why—vampires haven't killed people in two centuries. Why would they start with your dad?"

"I don't know why. But one did."

Even now, even after everything, she's still not convinced.

"Say I believe you, you have to see where they're coming from, Naz. You grew up with stories of vampires, more vivid than any of us have heard. It's logical that you would think the person who killed your father was a monster. Particularly as you witnessed it."

A new sense of anger ignites in me.

"Is this why you've come over? To tell me I'm crazy too, just like the rest of them think I am?"

"No. I'm trying to make you see why it would be normal for you to think vampires were involved."

"I don't think, Rey. I know. I saw it. Jesus, how many times do I have to say it?"

The relief and happiness I'd felt when I first saw her has quickly evaporated. Of course she's on Oliver and Jessop's side, thinking vampires can do no wrong.

"When are you going to stop searching for who you are?" I ask, turning the conversation around to her. "You said it yourself. You've only got the one party trick. Perhaps you're not a real witch at all. Perhaps it's just something freaky about that particular spell, and you're actually completely normal and should stop trying to find other witches and grimoires."

Her face crumples into a frown. "You know only a witch would be able to cast that spell."

"No, I don't. I don't know that at all. There aren't any witches to ask. The vampires—you know, the creatures you're convinced don't ever kill anyone—killed them all. Remember? For all we know, maybe it was an anti-spell."

"And anti-spell?" she asks, her forehead now furrowed in confusion.

"You know, something designed so that only non-witches can do it, to separate them from real witches."

"You can't believe that."

"Why not? You don't have any other evidence that you're a witch at all." I step forwards, take her hands and drop the attitude. "The thing is, you don't need anything more. You know in your heart of hearts that you are more than just that single spell. You know that when you get your hands on a grimoire, it will prove you right. And everyone else believes that, too. They wouldn't have kicked you out of Blackwatch if they didn't. I don't understand why it's not the same for me. Rey, I saw him. I saw the vampire with my own eyes. And I know, if I can just find him again…"

Dropping her hands, I turn back around and face the window.

"Do you know what? It doesn't even matter if no one else believes me. It's the truth. And when I find him, it will prove I was right all along. I have to find him, Rey. Surely you, of all people, understand that?"

There are tears in her eyes now, too. Tears that she wipes away with the back of a hand before nodding slowly.

"I do, I get it." She gently wraps her arms around me

again. "Maybe there's something I can do to help. But first, let's see if I can find a potion to encourage these bones to heal a bit quicker."

"What?'" I say pulling away from her. "You can do potions?"

"I'm not an entirely useless witch you know."

18

While Rey pulls out the contents of her plastic bag in my kitchen area, I try to make myself comfy with a few extra pillows from the bedroom.

"How are you able to do potions?" I ask. "You told me you could still only do that one spell."

"One spell, yes. Potions are different."

"They are? How?"

She looks across from the worktop. "You really want me to go into that now?"

"Why not. It might distract me from the cluster fuck that is my life."

"Fair enough. And I'm not going to disagree with you there, but you did bring this latest bit of crap on yourself."

"Look, are you going to talk to me about the witchy stuff or just do an Oliver and keep reminding me of all the terrible choices I've made?"

"Fine. Witchy stuff. But you have to bear in mind that pretty much everything I've learned has come from the internet, and ninety-nine percent of the stuff there is bullshit. An even higher percentage when it comes to magic. But there are a few useful tips I've picked up. The main thing about magic is that it's just energy. Plain, old, everyday energy."

"You know I despised physics at school, right?"

"I'm pretty sure most people hated physics. Okay, so bear with me for a quick recap then. When you did physics, you learned about different types of energy. Sound energy, light energy, chemical energy—that's in your food—that type of thing."

"Sounds vaguely familiar," I lie. The only thing worse than physics was history, but at least that teacher would leave you alone if you put your head on the desk and fell asleep at the back of the room. My physics teacher was a nightmare. She'd walk around the classroom, pen in her hair, always asking questions or pairing us up to do experiments that never worked. Still, I try to suppress these memories as Rey continues.

"Okay, so as a human, we can transfer and interpret certain types of energy. For example, our bodies chemically transfer the energy from our food into heat energy. Our muscles use this to provide movement. Our eyes and ears can interpret light and sound energy. But then there are a whole range of energies that we're just not accessing or using. That doesn't mean it can't be done. Sharks can interpret electrostatic energy, for example. We can't do that, but we know it's possible. Reindeer can see ultraviolet light. They can actually see things that are invisible to humans. But to reindeer, they're as clear as anything. Crazy right?"

"While I appreciate the science lesson, haven't you

gone off track a little here? I thought you were explaining about potions and why you can do more magic than you said."

"You're right. I'm just trying to give you context, that's all."

"Context appreciated. Can you move on?"

Her face falls by just a fraction. "Really? Because I've got some seriously cool facts about birds and snakes that tell you even more."

My look says it all.

"Fine then. Magic. Witches are able to harness other energies. Like the hidden energy in all the everyday objects around us. Not to mention the energy in air and water and earth."

"You can harness energy from air?"

"Of course I can't. I can't do anything. All the instructions for doing that are hidden in the grimoires. Really, the more I look into it, the fact I can do *one* spell without training is ridiculous. I guess my energy must be weirdly aligned with glass, or maybe one of its components, like sand."

"Well, you can be quite abrasive," I offer.

She groans. Rightly so. I think that is probably the worst Dad-type joke I have ever told but, sometimes, when they are that easy, you have no choice.

"Anyway, if we mix the right ingredients together, we can find elements that enhance each other's energies."

"So, potions are basically old-wives'-tales remedies?"

She laughs. "Kind of. But who's to say those old wives weren't witches? Also, I have to be honest here, you're kind of going to be a test subject for me. I've tried them on myself before, but I think maybe the witch part of me affects how they work. Adds extra energy or something. I don't know. I'm guessing now, but I think it works like that. We can find out, if you're willing to try."

For the first time, I pay a little more attention to the contents of her bag, which are now strewn out on my kitchen counter.

"Are you adding anything poisonous to it?"

"Of course not."

"What about onions? You know I don't like the taste of raw onions."

"There are no onions in it. It's mostly herbs. Fresh herbs, a few spices and flowers. Non-poisonous ones," she quickly adds.

I sniff the air although, from that distance, I can't smell anything at all.

"Fine," I say, slumping back down onto the sofa. "Whatever. It's not like my day can get any worse."

"Excellent," she grins. "Do you have any measuring scales?"

"No."

"Okay, never mind. I'll just guesstimate."

"Wow, that's reassuring," I say. "We're really off to a flying start.'

While Rey busies herself in the kitchen, I flick through my phone. Unsurprisingly, there's nothing from Oliver, or Calin. Maybe I should go back to his flat when I can walk a bit better. Calin's that is. Explain myself. Although what I'd say, I have no idea.

After half an hour, Rey walks over with a mug of what looks like tea, although it sure as hell doesn't smell like it. At best it smells like some weird herbal tea. At worst, well, let's not go there.

"How much of this do I have to drink?" I ask, scrunching up my nose.

"I'm not sure. Why don't you finish it and then we'll see if you need any more after that?"

Considering I was hoping she'd say two or three sips, her response is pretty disappointing. Picking up the steaming drink, I'm tempted to hold my nose, but only lifting one arm is painful enough. I'm not sure I could manage both.

"It's cooled for a while, so it should be fine to drink," she says, trying to be encouraging.

There's no way of putting this off. Still, I start with the smallest possible sip.

"Is there alcohol in this?" I ask, when something hits the back of my throat.

"Nope, but a ton of liquorice."

Liquorice is definitely not what I'm tasting but, considering the smell, it's not half as bad as I'd expected. Bracing myself, I finish the rest in several, large gulps. When I put the mug down, she's looking at me expectantly.

"So?" she asks. "Did it work? Does it feel better?"

"Is it meant to be instant?"

"I've really no idea. I made it once before, after I twisted my ankle on a run. It healed pretty quickly, but I was taking loads of ibuprofen too. Why don't I get you another mug? There's loads more in the saucepan."

"Let's give this half an hour or so first."

With a small shrug, she agrees, although it's less than thirty seconds before she's asking again.

"What about now? Does it feel any better now?"

Just to keep her happy, I attempt to lift my arm above

my head. There's still a whole heap of pain, though I actually manage to move it far higher than I would have thought.

"I'm not sure. Maybe," I say. Then, knowing that she's going to ask me every thirty seconds for the next three hours unless we can find something else to talk about, a thought springs to mind. Something I've been pondering for quite a while. And by a while, I mean at least five years.

"You know, if I had managed it? If I'd managed to find and kill the vampire, what would've happened to me? Would I be handed over to them? To their Council."

Her eyes widen. Obviously, this wasn't the direction she expected the conversation to take.

"I don't know, but I suspect not. I'm pretty sure it would be left to Blackwatch. I know when they were working out the Blood Pact, when the witches wouldn't agree and the vampires retaliated, it was the VC that dealt with their own. They cover anything that vampires do wrong. Blackwatch deals with the humans."

"And the witches?"

She offers a short snort of derision. "Well, that's a moot point now," she replies.

Not wanting to let her start dwelling on her own impossible quest, I recall a comment from before we got started on the topic of potions. "What did you mean, when you said you might be able to help?" I ask, sitting up straight with only minimal agony.

"What? You mean with the potion?"

"No, when we were talking about the vampires. When you first arrived, and I said how I had to track him down. I had to find him. You said you might be able to help. Do you still have information on them? From Blackwatch?"

She purses her lips, as she avoids my eyes, and when she opens her mouth to speak, she closes it again almost instantly.

"It was nothing," she says, finally meeting my gaze. "A stupid idea. A waste of time."

"What is?" I ask. "What are you talking about?"

She purses her lips yet again, leaning forwards ever so slightly before she speaks.

"Okay, but you have to promise me that this will not get back to Oliver."

19

"I don't think you should come. You don't need to come; I can do this on my own."

"We've been over this. Of course I'm coming. It'll be fine."

"In what world is a witch walking into a nest of vampires *fine?*"

It's been a week since my run-in with Joe, and I've not heard a single word from Oliver or Calin. I've tried sending a few messages to the former but, so far, I've had nothing in response. Rey keeps telling me to be patient. Apparently, he's a fraction less furious. I know she's right, but I miss him. On the plus side, my ribs and ankle are completely fine. I'm serious. Not even a twinge. So much for me being sceptical about Rey's potion. Obviously, she's the real deal when it comes to this whole witchiness thing.

Fortunately, we've had another topic of discussion to keep us occupied.

"I've already told you," she fires up her usual protest.

"The Blood Bank is not a nest. Blackwatch banned nests."

"It's just a regular place where vampires get together to drink human blood?"

"Which is provided for them, and monitored, by Blackwatch. You can't honestly think they'd let anything unsafe continue all this time."

There are a lot of things I think about Blackwatch, but I manage to hold my tongue. Since the first time she mentioned the Blood Bank, it's been almost all I can think about. I'd go so far as to say I have fantasised about it. In an ideal world, he'd be there, lurking in the shadows, slurping on a plastic bag of blood, ready for me to stake. Maybe I'd give him the chance to say something. To tell me why he'd done it, why he'd murdered my father. Then again, maybe I'd just pierce his heart before he has a chance to utter another word. That's the ideal scenario: find him, stake him and finally move on with my life, although I realise how unlikely that is. Still, even if he's not there when I visit the Blood Bank for the first time, who's to say I can't go back? Every week, every month, every year, if need be. I've been dedicated to this for so long, I'm not quitting now. Besides, if he's not there, other vampires might be able to point me in the right direction. After all, there can't be that many with skin and a scar like his.

But this is my fight, and the last thing I want to do is put Rey in any danger. If they get even the slightest inkling as to what she is, who knows how it could end. Unfortunately, we've found ourselves at an impasse, and she's the one with the upper hand.

"I've told you, I'm not going to tell you where the place is, so either I come with you or you don't go."

"You're being ridiculous," I tell her, for what feels like the hundredth time. "And you're contradicting yourself. *Again*. If Blackwatch has got this place as monitored as you say it is, then there shouldn't be any issue with me going in by myself."

"Oh, I don't think there's anything wrong with the average human walking into there. Someone you can guarantee will act rationally. But I'm afraid, Naz darling, that is not you. Seriously, tell me in all honesty what you would do if you found him?" she asks, eyebrows raised, looking down her nose at me. "Would you call Blackwatch? Or Oliver? Or me? No, of course you wouldn't. You've probably already been fantasising about stabbing him right there and then, in front of everyone, haven't you?"

At this point, I'm forced to look away. I thought I'd have been able to wear her down by now, but she's only getting more stubborn. Pretty soon, I'm going to have to face the fact that it's going to be her way or not at all. With a reluctant sigh, I fold my arms, and give it some serious consideration. I guess she knows the risks better than I do.

"Okay. Say I do let you tag along. You said it's all blood bags. How are we supposed to get in? Pretend we've got a delivery? Would that work? I don't suppose you've got your Blackwatch ID still handy, have you?"

She laughs off the comment, before biting down on her bottom lip.

"I didn't say it's only blood bags." A knowing smile spreads across her face. "Grey and I only did the drop once, when Jessop was away, but I saw on the requisitions list that there were live donors too."

"So, we go in as donors?"

"Exactly. There are all sorts of rules Blackwatch has about consent, so we don't actually have to let one of them feed from us. Unless you've got a taste for it now?"

The remark is clearly a dig about Calin but, being the mature adult that I am, I stay silent, and she realises she's not going to get a rise out of me and carries on.

"So, what do you think? Shall we get all dressed up and hang out in a bar full of undead bastards and try and track down your dad's killer?"

Two near-death experiences in the space of a couple of weeks should really have taught me a lesson. But what's the old saying? *The third time's a charm?*

"I guess I ought to get changed," I say with a grin.

"Yes," she replies, pointedly staring at a ketchup stain on my pyjama top. "You really ought to."

20

I don't know if it's the witch in her or whether she just has nerves of freaking steel, but I swear she looks as cool as anything in her black boots and leather jacket, striding towards this big old warehouse. I, on the other hand ... well. Maybe it's the fact that I've spent this whole journey concealing a nine-inch, wooden stake inside the lining of my jacket. Obviously, I can't let Rey know about it, so she naturally assumes my nervousness is all about the Blood Bank.

"It'll be fine," she says. "There's always a member of the VC there to oversee things. Just follow my lead. Let me do all the talking."

"Do you think they'll search us before we're allowed in?"

"Search us? Why?"

"I don't know. Maybe make sure we don't have any weapons on us or anything?"

I keep looking straight forwards as I speak. She pulls up.

"Naz," she says, accusingly.

"What?"

"Don't make me regret this."

"I'm just asking, that's all."

I resist the urge to place my hand on the concealed stake. It should be fairly straight forward to plough it through a dead sternum. And I'd be lying if I said I hadn't practised. At some point, someone is going to move the wardrobe in my old flat and think I was rehearsing for a remake of the Shawshank Redemption.

It's taken us almost an hour to get here. Even if Rey had relented and given me directions, I doubt I'd have been able to find it on my own. The storage park we've arrived at is just a short train ride from Wimbledon, but it's a world away from grassy tennis courts and strawberries and cream. The buildings are clad with corrugated iron and have tin roofs. Rusted fence posts stand guard, broken chains dangling. You can tell it's the type of place that always looks grey. Even in daylight. There are about a dozen cars parked on the oil-stained tarmac. Less than half of them look like they would actually be drivable. Mixed among them are a few caravans, propped up on bricks, with silhouettes moving at the windows.

This is definitely a place you'd avoid on a dark night. The type of place you'd avoid at any time of day, in fact. Yet we're walking towards it.

"Are you sure this is it?" I ask, currently feeling strangely grateful that my first conventional vampire experience was in a luxury flat in Mayfair. Somehow, I don't think I'd have been quite so willing to take Joanna's place and come here on my own. Fortunately, I'm not on my own. Rey's with me and she knows what she's doing. At least, she looks like she does.

"Don't worry," she says. "I know what you're thinking. It's not much further now."

"But it's here? In a storage park?"

"I don't know exactly, but this is where we dropped the blood off."

Something has been bothering me about this whole Blood Bank thing. Something I've been wanting to ask her all night, but given that we've been on public transport and surrounded by people the whole time, I've not really had a chance. But, right now, it's just us and I feel I have to know, before we go any further.

"How do Blackwatch manage to keep this place a secret?" I ask her, hearing my voice louder than I intend. "Donating blood individually, to one or two vampires, is one thing but, surely, if people see a whole bar full, they're going to tell someone? Surely they'll go to the police or something."

Rey offers a slight hum of consideration, as she continues walking.

"I guess it's a mix of things, really. The VC likely pays enough for discretion. Certainly the ones who come here fork out a lot for the privilege. But I also suspect the volunteers they get are not the type who would be believed if they did report it. Sad but true."

My thoughts go back to Joanna. She's right. You don't get people volunteering their bodies if they've got better options in life. You get the ones who are struggling, who have no other choice. I can't imagine how bad their lives must be to be brought to this. I don't want to, either. And I know that probably makes me a bad person.

"Okay, see that door up ahead, in the front of the warehouse, with the woman standing there? That's our entrance."

I stare through the night to where she's pointing. In the shadow of a busted-up 4x4, I can just make out a figure. A new fear winds its tentacles around my chest.

"Rey, if we go in there, are they going to feed from us?" The thought of dozens of those dagger-like fingernails clawing at my skin is almost enough to make me stop in my tracks.

"I don't know. Maybe. But, remember, it's only the exceptionally wealthy vampires that can afford the donors, most of them will be drinking out of bags."

Exceptionally wealthy, like Calin, I think; although I don't reckon a vampire who can afford a flat like his would choose to hang out somewhere like this. My stomach begins to churn, and I feel nerves starting to get the better of me. This is ridiculous, I tell myself. This is what I want. This is what I've always wanted—to be in a room with dozens of vampires, so that I can finally pinpoint the one that killed my dad. And, like Rey said, nothing's going to happen. Blackwatch would never let anything untoward occur. As the possibilities of what we're about to face race through my imagination, another thought suddenly springs to mind. One that actually does cause me to stop dead.

"What about you? Have you done it before? Have you ever had one feed from you?"

Ray stops, two steps ahead, and waits a moment before turning back to face me. Her eyes are angled slightly down.

"Once. It happened once."

"Wow. I didn't know that."

"No, well, it's not something I tell people. It was part of recruitment. How far would I go and still hold my nerve?"

"And you went …"

"All the way. Fangs in the neck. It wasn't a long feed, and the vampire was really lovely afterwards, to be fair. I get it. It's something Blackwatch needs to do, to test we're committed. Plus, it's important. We can't expect others to sign up to being donors, if we're not even willing to experience it for ourselves."

In the short silence that follows, dots join up in my brain, to form a logical extension to her statement. "That mean's Oliver …" I can't even finish the sentence.

"Yup, all of us," she confirms my unfinished conclusion. "Some of the guys still do it regularly, too. It's not exactly encouraged, but it's not frowned upon either. Of course, they don't come here."

"Wow, I didn't realise that it was such a lovefest between Blackwatch and the vamps."

"Come on, let's get this over with."

She reaches back, grabs my hand and drags me along. In another setting, we'd look like any regular pair of girls about to hit up a club which, I suppose, in a way, we are.

With more than enough to think about, we fall silent as we walk in sync across the potholed carpark, trying to avoid the puddles. I'm in the same dress I wore that second time for Calin, the only thing that felt suitable, but my hair is tied up, and my battered, leather jacket conceals the stake. As we approach the broken-down 4x4, the woman turns to face us.

"What are you doing here?" she asks. Her voice is deep and velvety and I can tell in an instant that she is definitely another vampire and definitely not the one who killed my dad. "This is private property."

"We know. Blackwatch sent us."

We decided earlier that Rey would do the talking, which is great as I can't stop staring at the woman. It's not that she's perfect by any stretch. I've seen plenty of living women far more beautiful, well at least looking more beautiful after they've been Photoshopped to death on the cover of a magazine. But she's so … so … alluring. Yes, that's the word. Her eyes flick between the pair of us.

"We've already got our three donors for the night. They arrived two hours ago."

"I know." Rey doesn't miss a beat. "But someone called Blackwatch and said there was likely to be an influx of, what did he call them? Governors? Councillors, I don't know the term. But he said they needed a couple more of us, last minute."

The vampire's eyes widen.

"More members of the Council?"

"Maybe? Yeah, I think that's what he said. Members of the Council. They wanted to make sure there were plenty of us to go around."

The vampire frowns. Well, her face moves into the closest thing to one. No wrinkles actually form. Any woman who thinks Botox is the answer to unwanted frown lines should definitely give vampirism a try. Maybe there's a business plan in there for someone.

"Have you been here before?" She looks at both of us as she speaks.

"I have," Rey answers. "About two years ago. But I have a regular now. He's planning on coming along too. She's new though." She nods her head in my direction, at which point the vampire also offers a knowing dip of the chin. "She's only done solo work before."

"That would explain the heart rate," she says. "Okay then, nothing's changed in the last couple of years. You stick to the holding rooms, down the stairs and to the right. If you head into the bar, it's on you. The Blood Pact is void in there."

"We know," Rey says confidently. "Holding rooms only."

Rather than turning to the door behind her, which is what we were both expecting, the vampire walks between us, to a dirty patch of ground, where she reaches down and heaves open a hatch door.

I hear a gasp from Rey as a long, narrow staircase is revealed. Thumping, bass music reverberates up to us.

Underground. The Blood Bank is underground.

"Well, this changes things a little bit," I whisper.

21

Okay, so this is not going to plan. So much for a small storage facility and a few vampires having a quiet drink together. Right now, anything is possible. Stepping past the vampire bouncer towards the staircase, it's impossible to control my heart rate. Underground? We are about to go into an underground vampires' nest? Jesus Christ Naz! If I didn't believe Oliver before when he said I had some kind of death wish, I'm starting to now.

Fighting the urge to reach for the stake, I follow Rey. I must have only taken ten steps down, when a voice comes from above.

"Have a nice night, ladies," she calls. A moment later, the hatch falls shut with an ominous thump. Like the closing of a coffin lid.

Red wall lights offer a dim glow as we begin our descent. As dark as the place is, it's a darn sight cleaner than on the outside—not a hint of dirt on the metal steps or on the handrail, which I'm gripping far tighter than is probably necessary. For the first moment or so, Rey and I are utterly silent, and it takes me a moment to realise we must have already walked down over twenty steps. I begin to wonder just how far underground we're going. Two flights? Three flights? Maybe this leads to some abandoned tube station. That's what it feels like, at least. Maybe there's a whole network of tunnels under here that vampires can travel through during daylight hours. I'm probably letting my imagination run a bit wild now, but it would make sense. They've probably got enough money. The drumming we heard from the top of the stairs is getting progressively louder. Low and steady, like a heartbeat

"What do we do?" I ask, finally. "I thought you said it was in a storage container. Small. Easy exit. How are we going to get out, now it's underground?"

"Shh, I'm thinking."

Biting on my lip, I force myself to stay silent, although it's not easy. We didn't have a choice; Rey knows that as well as I do. If we'd refused to go down the staircase, the vampire upstairs would have known something was wrong. They'd probably call Blackwatch to check us out, and then they'd send people. Fine by me, another lecture on disappointment from Jessop, but for Rey … not so much. Best case scenario, Jessop kicks her arse back to the nineteen-nineties. Worse case, the vampires somehow find out what she is.

It's not just the dungeonesque vibe about the place that's giving me the heebie-jeebies. I really want to keep the thought to myself. I know Rey's got enough to worry about, as we head into a possibly inescapable hole, with creatures hell-bent on ridding the world of witches, but I can't help myself.

"No Blood Pact agreement," I say, as we continue on downward. "That was what she said, Rey. You heard that, right? I thought that was, like, an international law."

"It is, she's just trying to scare us, that's all. If the vamps tried anything, even here, they'd know there would be hell to pay."

"You're sure?"

"I'm sure. You think Blackwatch would still send donors if they were being murdered? You think they'd still give them blood bag donations? Of course they wouldn't. It's just to stop us from wandering around and sticking our noses where they don't belong."

Exactly like we're planning on doing, although I'm not feeling half as confident as I was before. And I wasn't feeling all that confident to start with. I'll be honest, I'm not a great fan of being underground, and this has caught me off guard. I'm not even a massive fan of tube stations. Just something about having tonnes and tonnes of earth above me sends me into an unnaturally cold sweat. I'm the type of person that's born to stay above ground. I realise that probably sounds strange, but that's how I feel whenever I'm somewhere like this.

"What's this about holding rooms?" I ask, trying to divert my mind from an increasing sense of claustrophobia. "Are we kept in cages?"

"I don't know. I guess so."

"You guess so?"

"I just dropped off the blood bags last time I was here, remember. I never came downstairs. I don't know all the ins and outs. Look, I realise you're not their biggest fan, but you need to trust Blackwatch and the Blood Pact right now. Vampires aren't allowed to get carried away. If a donor tells them they have to stop, they have to stop."

"They do?"

"They do."

"Even here."

"Everywhere."

Well, I didn't know that. No wonder Calin got carried away. I was too busy keeping my mouth shut and letting him feed. He probably thought I was fine.

"This may be a dodgy location," she continues. "But these are all regular, every-day vampires. Remember, ninety-nine percent of them have entirely normal jobs. Dentists, CEOs, politicians."

"You know you have literally just listed the most sadistic professions available to man," I tell her.

"Yeah, maybe those weren't the best examples, but you get my point. It doesn't matter where we are. Being underground, it's fine. It doesn't change anything."

The drumming is now so loud that it's drowning out my footsteps, and as we take the last couple of stairs, we find ourselves at a large, metal door. The nerves that have been multiplying in my chest are now joined by a tremor of anticipation. This could really be it. This could really be the night I find my father's killer.

Rey reaches back and squeezes my hand, before glancing over her shoulder to offer me a tentative grin.

"Are you ready for this?" she asks. "We could find another way? Ask Oliver?"

"Oliver's not going to help me and you know it. What

about you? Are you okay? I can do this alone. If you want to go back upstairs, I'd understand."

She shakes her head emphatically, like she couldn't even consider leaving me.

"Then I'm ready as I'm ever going to be."

"In that case, welcome to the Blood Bank."

22

If I'd thought the music was loud before, I was mistaken. Vampires, it turns out, love epic speaker systems and apparently have no concern for their ear drums or auditory health. As the door swings open, we're hit by a wall of smoke and sound, both eye watering in their own right.

"Jesus," I say, covering my eyes, as I choke on the fumes. "I guess you don't have to worry about the effects of tar or nicotine when you're already dead."

My voice is drowned out and Rey is already two steps ahead of me, standing in a dimly lit corridor. Straight ahead, it continues on into blackness. To the right, is another corridor, where we were told we would find the holding rooms, a single strip light buzzing on the ceiling. Rey, however, is facing to the left and looking through a narrow archway. With the stinging in my eyes just about under control, I blink away the tears, before lifting my gaze and finally taking in the scene there. The cavernous space reveals something totally unexpected. *This* is the Blood Bank?

I don't know what I had actually expected, coming to a vampire bar. I guess I thought I'd be walking into something fairly standard. You know, a few tables, some people chatting. Perhaps a pool table, where a couple of the eternal undead could shoot a few games, while mulling over their day at the office. So, essentially, I'd expected a normal bar, just with vampires. This—and believe me, there is no other way to describe it—is a pit of sheer debauchery.

I edge my way forwards, peering over Rey's shoulder to the space beyond her. From what I can see, there is no bar, just half-a-dozen or so massive fridges, with glass fronts, all filled, or half filled, with gleaming red bags. There are tables, a complete mishmash of them, ranging from the plastic garden variety to sleek glass dining tables and everything else in between. And the chairs are just as eclectic. The ceiling here is higher and bizarrely, the lighting comes from a mock chandelier. Made of cast iron and intricately fashioned with swirls and loops, it would look seriously gothic if it were not for the modern-day lightbulbs fitted in it. But, obviously, it's not the decor of the space that holds my attention half as much as the creatures occupying it. To be fair to my original assumption, one or two do appear to be sitting around, sipping the contents of the bags through straws and having a perfectly normal conversation. But it really is just one or two of them. Mostly, if they're not participating in it, then they're watching the show. Or, should I say, shows.

I can't tell from where I'm standing, how far the space extends, but it's obvious there must be dozens of nooks and crannies and, in every corner I can see, there's more feeding going on. So much for Blackwatch sending three or four humans. There's at least a dozen, all in various stages of undress. My attention is drawn to a guy of similar age to me, who is currently spread out on a long, wooden table with four vampires feeding from him. I can't imagine how painful that must be, even with the venom, but he seems a long way from caring. His head is hanging off the edge of the table, as he arches his back, his eyes wide and rolling, and his mouth is open as he groans.

"Blackwatch knows about *this*?" I ask, my eyes moving to another part of the room, where three bodies—whether they're human or vampire I can't even tell—are tangled together in a corner.

"No," she replies, her eyes locked on the scene in front of us. "They can't. These donors aren't from Blackwatch. It's against the rules for more than one vampire to feed from a human at the same time."

"Then where?"

I hear a short, sharp hiss. If it wasn't for the bloody music, I suspect I'd be able to hear her teeth grinding together, too.

"Best guess? They are neophytes."

"Neophytes?"

"Neophytes commit to a particular vampire. They do whatever it wants, in the hope that, at some point, they'll be turned. After the Blood Pact, they were outlawed for essentially being a form of slavery. It's not legal. Not even close."

She gestures with a slight nod to a corner of the room, where a girl is dangling a blood bag above the head of an older grey-haired vampire, while he kneels on the floor with a dog collar around his neck. I quickly look away.

"See that one over there? She was on the Blackwatch books as a donor for about a year, when I was there. Was happy to do all sorts of clients. But then she stopped requesting work. Said she'd saved up enough money to buy a house, or was moving to France, or something, but I guess she had other plans. Stupid woman."

"On the plus side, at least she's found a guy who's not afraid of commitment," I say. It's just a quip, an attempt to lighten the mood, but Rey doesn't see it that way.

"It's bloody dangerous, is what it is. Not to mention the fact that it will never happen. She will never become a vampire. Vampires are imprisoned for decades for turning humans without it being sanctioned by the Vampire Council. Plus, any vamp who'll work around Blackwatch procedures to feed is not one you can trust."

My mind goes instantly to Calin. Would he have taken up my offer to cut Blackwatch out of our arrangement? And what would that say about him if he did? Realising that I have more important issues to consider right now, I bring myself back to the moment.

'Okay, time to get in there," I say.

"What?"

"Well, the sooner we get in, the sooner we get out."

The adrenaline in my body has switched from flight to fight mode. If I'm going to find him, I'm going to need to take a proper look. Not wanting to stay down here any longer than necessary, I take a step towards the throng, only to have Rey grab my arm.

"Wait. The vamp upstairs said we should go to a holding room. We need to take a right here."

"I need to find this vampire."

"Naz, slow down and think. Let's try and keep the risk as low as we can."

"Considering we're in a nest of vampires, you mean?"

She doesn't reply. Instead, she pulls me around and tries to drag me down the other corridor. I resist.

"Rey, I need to do this."

She shakes her head. "Not yet. We need to think this through. We can't just go in there. We need to stick to the plan. Check all doors and exits, before you go looking. That needs to stay the same. This is bigger than I thought. Bigger than Blackwatch …" She lets the rest of her sentence trail into the air. "Vampires have to stick to the Blood Pact, but if they are willing to feed like these, who knows …"

The fact that Blackwatch might hide something like this has got her spooked. I can see it in her face. And I want to offer her support. I want to be the same amazing friend to her that she has been to me. But in the pit of my stomach, I know he's in there somewhere. Maybe in one the areas that branch off to the side. One good look, that's all I need. And my feet are itching to move.

"Rey?"

"Please, Naz. Let's just see, okay. Maybe we don't need to go in there. Maybe there's another way."

My eyes go back to the dozens of vampires, smoking and dancing and laughing into the night. I'm so close, I know I am. But what do I do? I turn and face her.

"Okay, let's revise the plan," I say.

23

The stupidity of working out a new plan, halfway through this crazy escapade, is not lost on me, but I'll call it adapting. From what Rey knew about the Blood Bank, she had assumed it was upstairs in one of the large warehouses. We had also assumed it would be a slightly more civilised affair. Right now, we are left with two options: head back up the stairs having gained nothing, and possibly invoke the suspicions of the vampire guard up top; or wait it out down here until a better idea comes to us.

It's hard to tear my eyes away from the scenes in front of me, when every bone in my body is telling me that's what I need to do, but it only takes a few paces to reach our authorised location. Holding cell is right. Dusty and grime-covered, with large metal bars on the open door. Perhaps it's been here since the war, although the bars seem too new for that. Maybe Blackwatch designed the whole thing to look like this. I wouldn't put it past them.

Inside the cell, one guy and two girls are sitting on a

wooden bench. The guy has a vampire feeding from his neck, the other two seem pretty bored. One of them is painting her nails a garish purple, while the other one is just picking at hers.

"Okay," Rey whispers to me. "I guess this is where we wait."

Taking a seat on the end of the bench, it's hard to ignore the slurping coming from the vampire at the opposite end. Every now and again, there's this smacking noise too, as he stops to lick his lips. While I don't know what traits follow from human to vampire, I'd be willing to guess this guy was one hell of a messy eater when he was still alive.

I've barely sat down when my feet start tapping on the floor.

"Rey," I begin.

"Look, just give it a minute. We've got a perfect view from here if he comes in or out. Just keep your eyes on the door."

"Assuming there's only one exit and entrance."

She doesn't reply to that. "This is not the time to start a conversation about that," she says eventually as she flicks her eyes towards the feeding vamp.

A few minutes pass. The music in the main room changes, by which I mean the heavy bass gets just a fraction slower. Finally, with one more disgusting slurp, the vampire stands up, shoves some money into the boy's hand and leaves. Five humans. Alone. Five humans and a whole mass of vampires only a stone's throw away. With a heavy sigh, the nail-picking girl looks across at us and speaks.

"Blackwatch send you?" she asks loudly, above the

din. She isn't exactly hostile, but I'm pretty certain we aren't about to become BFFs.

"Uh-huh," I reply, to which she both huffs and snorts simultaneously.

"For real? I can't believe they sent more people. Why the hell would they do that? There's hardly enough work as it is. You know we've only had three vamps in here the whole night."

"Three? That's all?" I ask.

"Yup."

"But it'll get busier, won't it? I mean, you must get more coming through here than that?"

She sniffs. "I doubt it. Been like this for the last few weeks."

Minimal vampire exposure is not what I'm after.

"But do you see the others? Do they walk past here at all?"

Her final response is a non-committal shrug, at which point she goes back to picking her nails, confirming that our conversation is over.

I bite down on my lip, knowing that there's probably some kind of etiquette when it comes to this type of place, kind of like being in a lift, where you avoid eye contact, try your best to maintain everyone's personal space and definitely don't speak to anyone, ever. But I've come here for a reason and I don't have time for convention.

"You guys been here before?" I ask, adjusting my position so I can speak to the other two, who nod.

"Great, I wonder if you could help me then. I'm looking to find a particular vampire." Reaching into my jacket pocket, I pull out one of my sketches. It's not the best I've ever done, and it's three or four years old, but I feel I got this one right with the details. Like the scar above his eyebrow and the way his lip curls up on one side. "Have you seen a guy that looks like this?" I unfold it and offer it out.

"Jesus, Naz!" Rey snatches back the paper before one of the others can get a proper look. "What the hell are you doing with that? What would you have done if the vamp upstairs had found it on you?"

"Well, assuming she knew who it was," I say as I snatch my drawing back, "I'd have asked her for a name."

She is pissed off; I can see it in her face. "That's not what we agreed. We agreed you would come down here to look. That's all. Not hand out bloody fliers to attract everyone's attention."

"I'm trying to find a damn murderer."

The words come out a little louder than I'd intended, causing the others in the cell to shift further back against the wall.

"Vampires don't kill people," one of the girls says, but with a quiver of uncertainty in her voice.

"Yeah? Well this one did. I saw it myself." I thrust the picture in her direction again. Her eyes barely glance at it before she shakes her head.

"Never seen him," she says.

"What about you?" I stretch the picture over to the girl who's painting her nails.

She offers the same, cursory glance. "Nope."

I don't feel like there's much point even asking the guy, he seems a little too out of it, but before I can sit back down again, he plucks it out of my hand.

"I've seen him. Yeah, I'm sure I have. Early thirties, right? Low voice."

His answer catches me by surprise.

"I didn't hear him speak but yeah, early thirties. You've seen him here?"

"A couple of times."

"And he feeds from the donors?"

"Sometimes. He's not fed from me, personally, but I've seen him in here. I think he mostly just goes into the bar, though. Drinks from all the vamp lovers a lot, too."

My heart starts skipping. He's been here. He might be here now.

"Have you seen him tonight?" I walk over to the entrance to our cell, peering down the corridor towards the bar. "What time does he usually come and feed? When did you last see him?"

"Hey, you need to slow down." The guy lifts his palms to me. "I said I recognised him. I didn't say I knew his daily schedule."

"But recently, have you seen him recently?"

It's not just my heart that's racing now. My feet have graduated from tapping, to pacing.

"I need to go in there." I say to myself more than anything else, but Rey is on her feet in an instant.

"You can't be serious? No! We've been through this."

"He said he feeds in there."

"He also said he comes in here. We have to wait. You must have patience."

"Patience." I stop my pacing and square up to her. "I've been patient, Rey. I have been patient for ten bloody years. What I need right now is revenge."

"You're not thinking straight."

"No, but I will be the moment I put a stake through his heart."

Dipping my hand inside my jacket, I pull out the piece of wood I've been concealing and hold it by my side. Rey's eyes widen and she steps back.

"Come on, Naz. What the hell are you thinking?"

"What do you think I'm thinking?"

I walk to the entrance, steel myself with a deep breath and tuck the stake up my sleeve, before turning back to my only friend.

"Look, you don't have to come with me. I get that it's a whole heap of risk for you, but I've wasted enough time. I can't get over this. I can't move past it. And whether he's in there or not, someone in there, maybe all of them, know who he is and where I can find him. I'm doing this Rey. I have to." I turn to the others on the bench. "Do we go out the same way we came in, or is there another exit?"

"Don't go up the stairs," the guy answers. "The vamp at the top is a bitch. Will leave you hammering against that hatch until your knuckles bleed before she'll let you out. Says she can't hear you which is crap, obviously. There's another exit, down the corridor opposite the main entrance. Just keep following it until you hit more stairs. It brings you out in one of the warehouses."

"And are there vampires waiting there? Do they use that exit too?"

He shakes his head. "No idea."

"Okay, that's great."

Turning back to Rey I take her hands.

"You go," I say to her.

"What? No. I'm not leaving you."

"Yes, you are. This isn't safe for you. They might be able to sense you. You know, sense what you are."

Her eyebrow's rise up to her hairline. "That's bullshit and you know it. No, I'm not leaving you. I've been around vampires a darn sight more than you, Naz."

It was bullshit, I was quite aware, but I'm clutching at straws which means the only option I'm left with is the truth.

"Please, Rey. I can't worry about you and find this guy at the same time. Take the other exit. Wait in the warehouse. If I'm not back in an hour," the words catch in my throat, "then call Oliver. Let him know about this place. Let him know it all. Say I blackmailed you. Say the potion you gave me drove me crazy and I kidnapped you. Anything, I don't care."

Even in the crappy lighting I can see her eyes starting to glisten, which is ridiculous because, honestly, I'll see her again in half an hour. But I know it's tough for her. She's always the person looking out for everyone else.

"Look," I say, forcing a grin. "This place is a win-win situation for me. Either I find Dad's killer or someone who knows him or I don't. Worst case scenario is I somehow get myself killed, in which case, you'll have all the evidence you need to prove that these guys are not the friendly bloodsuckers you've been trying to convince me they are. Now please, go!"

She blinks away the tears from her eyes and offers a short nod.

"I'll be waiting for you," she says.

24

Strange as it is, I actually feel better now that I'm on my own. I'm not going to pretend I know more about vampires than Rey and I suspect, if anything kicked off, she'd be able to defuse the situation much faster with her Blackwatch knowledge than my quick mouth would. But I can't worry about that. There's so much about them we don't understand. What exactly they can do. What they can sense. And, from what my dad and Oliver told me about the way they treated the witches ... well, it's better Rey's out of harm's way.

Taking a deep breath, I move away from the holding cell and head back towards the main room.

"I hope you're right about this Blood Pact agreement, Rey," I mutter under my breath, as the volume of the music increases.

Nothing much has changed since I looked in earlier. People have moved about a bit, that's all. The vamp wearing the dog collar is still on the ground, only his human counterpart now has a whip. By the looks of things, the guy on the table has passed out, or fallen asleep, as just a couple of vampires continue to lick at his puncture marks.

The floor is covered in cigarette butts and shredded plastic. With the quantity of blood bags these guys seem to get through, it would be nice to think they'd consider recycling – a weird thought to cross my mind right now, I'll admit, but I guess I'm just trying to rationalise the chaos around me. Not that I'm sure it can be rationalised. Trying to control my heartbeat, I step further in and shiver. That's when I notice how cold it is.

Normally, in a room packed like this, I'd be sweating from all the body heat generated. Even in winter, you should barely need any heating on with this many people crammed so close together. But not in here. Here it feels like the heat is actually being sucked out of the room. I tug my jacket a little tighter around me and scan the scene in front of me. *He's got to be here,* I repeatedly say to myself. *He's got to.* Thoughts of doing the deed cause the shivers to intensify. It will take less than a minute of my life. Then Blackwatch can turn up and do what they want with me. Stupid as it sounds, I'm completely fine with that. It can't be any worse than the prison my mind has been lately.

Refocusing my attention on the room, I'm surprised to notice that I've already passed the first fridge and I'm deep in the debauchery. So much for me worrying about being conspicuous. The fact that no one seems to care I'm here is a positive, although the size of the place is not. And now that I'm halfway across the room, I see another sight to make my stomach plummet even further;

another two freaking staircases—one leading up, and the other down.

"Shit," I mutter to myself. This place is like one of those crappy clubs I used to go to in my late teens, where every floor would have a different theme—pop music, or R&B or 80s grunge, that sort of thing. I wonder if it's the same for the way they feed here. Chilled blood, blood at room temperature, high-octane, dance-party blood. Given that I've not seen anyone who looks remotely like my guy, I know my only option is to check them out. Tightening my grip on the stake in my jacket, I reach the first staircase, the one heading up, but hesitate.

"Everything okay there? You seem lost. Are you looking for someone?"

It takes a second to realise that this is aimed at me. Still wondering what the hell my next move is going to be, I turn to the side, to find an older vampire looking directly at me. Her long, white hair falls across the front of one of her shoulders and down past her waist, braided like some Celtic priestess. She's sitting demurely at a low table and in her hand is a delicate teacup into which, it appears, she has decanted the contents of a blood bag.

"Can I help at all?" she asks, smiling, although it's difficult to decide whether this is meant to be encouraging or threatening. While she seems nice enough, it's hard not to feel nervous when you see the length of her fangs.

"I'm fine," I reply, in that intrinsically British way that we always do, regardless of whether we're actually okay or not.

"Well, let me know if I can help at all. I don't think I've seen you here before."

My instinct is to head up the staircase and keep searching but, as we're aware, my instincts aren't always great. So, instead, I change my mind and turn back to her. It should look out of place, an elderly looking lady, drinking blood from a teacup in a bar full of half-naked humans and vampires, but somehow it works.

"Actually, I'm looking for someone."

"Oh, yes?" With a flick of her tongue, she delicately removes a drop of blood from her lip. "And who might that be?"

My stomach starts to clench. "I don't know his name," I reply. At least I'm starting with the truth. "I met him through a friend. He asked me to come here."

"So, a man? What does he look like, dear? And where exactly did he ask you to meet him?"

Now my throat has started to tighten, and no amount of cold air could stop the sweating now making my palms slick. "Honestly, it's fine," I say, waving a hand. "I'm sure I'll find him soon enough."

"If you just tell me what he looks like, I'm sure I'll be able to help. Particularly if he's a regular. I have been coming here for a very long time." She adds a light-hearted chuckle, exposing her two top fangs, along with the gaps where the bottom ones once were. Again, I consider retreating, but there's the chance she can give me a name, in which case I'll be straight out of here and back to Rey. Hunting someone with a name attached has got to be infinitely easier. Besides, with more to go on, maybe Jessop would finally look into it properly.

"He's in his thirties," I start, realising age is probably not the best identifier for a vampire. "At least he looks like he is. And he's got a scar, just above his eyebrow, around here." I point to the position on my own face, and I'm about to continue on to describe his pitted skin, (although how I do that politely, I have no idea), when it turns out I don't need to. Her eyes narrow, as she places the teacup down on its saucer.

"What did you say your name was, dearie?" She smiles again, but now it's as cold as ice.

"I ... I didn't."

"No, you didn't."

She stands up. I'm ready to move away, but she's across from behind the table, before I can even blink.

"And where did you say you met this vampire?"

"I … uhm … through a friend. Another donor …"

"And they've been here before?"

"I … I …"

Instinctively, my fingers grasp for the stake. It's the most minuscule of movements, but she's on me, pushing me against the wall. She slips her hand inside my jacket and pulls out the piece of wood, all remnants of a smile gone.

"I think you should tell me exactly what you are doing here."

25

Her grip around my wrist is like a vice and I don't doubt for a second that she can sense my panic, increasing exponentially. Scanning the room, I try to think on my feet. Should I call for help? But what would I say? And to whom? The humans here are obviously fine with a bit of rough play, and she's got hold of my stake, for God's sake. So much for the sweet old lady act.

"What are you doing here?" she hisses at me, the metallic scent of blood thick on her breath.

"I told you, I'm looking for a vampire. He asked me to meet him here."

"I know you're lying. Even if I couldn't hear it from the pounding of that pathetic, little heart of yours, it's written all over your face. Besides, that vampire …" She sniffs at me. "You're not his type."

My heart is racing, to the point where I'm not even sure if it can keep going at this pace for much longer. Still, at the moment, none of the other vampires seem interested.

"Please, I just need to speak to him. Ask him something."

"What, with this?" She lifts the stake. "This is hardly a conversational aid. Please don't act the innocent with me, dearie."

She turns it over and over in her fingers, before pressing the sharpened tip against my cheek. I try to stifle the scream building inside me.

"Please … Please …"

"Oh yes, beg. I so enjoy it when you humans do that."

"I just want to know where I can find him."

"Who sent you?"

"No one sent me. I'm here by myself."

"Stop lying. Tell me, or I will snap your neck."

Her fingertips press down on my throat, blocking the air to my lungs.

"The Blood Pact," I manage to choke out.

Her eyes narrow. "Oh yes, the Blood Pact. How could I forget? It's a shame though, you know. People do have such terrible accidents. Particularly young girls, out late at night, on their own, in unsavoury parts of town. It really is quite tragic," she snorts, bringing her vile face closer to mine.

I feel her fangs graze my skin and the pressure on my throat is increasing. A few faces have turned in our direction now. The staircase beside us has become crowded with people, as they pause to enjoy the show.

"A name, please. If you're going to kill me, just tell me his name first. And let him know I came for him, like I promised."

"Wow, you are determined. Perhaps I was wrong. Maybe you would be Damien's type, after all."

Before she can elaborate, a distinct voice emerges above the murmur of the crowd, the words so furious that they cut through the music and freeze all conversation.

"Get your hands off her!"

"No," I gasp, as attention switches to Rey. "No!"

This time I manage to scream as, in the moment of confusion, I slip free of the vampire's grip. But I've barely gone half a step, before she grabs me by the wrist and yanks me back.

"This looks interesting," she says.

Rey moves out of the crowd and steps forwards. There's only one show going on now, and every human and every vampire has stopped to watch.

"I said let her go," she growls.

If I thought I was trembling before, it's nothing compared to now. Every muscle in my body is shaking with terror. If anyone was meant to be in any danger, it was me. This is *my* mission. *My* revenge. She should be all the way back to the surface by now, getting ready to call Oliver.

"Please, Rey. Just go," I plead, tears blinding me, as my friend continues to advance.

The vampire, at least, appears to be enjoying herself.

"What's the rush?" Still holding me by the wrist, she drags me behind her. "This another one of your friends, here by *invitation?* Isn't that something? Well, the more the merrier, I say."

Every pair of eyes, human or otherwise, are now on us, but either Rey can't see it, or she just doesn't care. I get the feeling it's the latter.

"I've asked you twice now," she says, her voice as

calm as if she's enquiring about the price of a pint of milk. "This will be the last time. Now, please. Let. Her. Go."

If it wasn't for the fact that she's gripping my wrist so tightly that it could easily break, I'd think the old vampire had forgotten about me. Her eyes are locked on Rey.

"That's hardly a very persuasive argument, young lady. I'm not exactly sure what you think you're going to do in this situation. You see, you're a little outnumbered. And, I hate to tell you, underprepared." With a snarl, she bares her fangs and several of the nearby humans, myself included, shrink back.

"Don't you worry," Rey replies, now standing directly in front of her. "I'm completely prepared."

Her eyes begin to burn with a light so intense, that even the vampires stiffen. Then her lips start to move and, in that moment, I know what's going to come out of her mouth. I know what she's going to say, to reveal. The sacrifice she's about to make.

"No!" With a force I didn't know I possessed, I yank my wrist out of the old woman's grip and throw myself towards my friend. "No Rey! Don't!"

But it's too late.

"*Suh-doh-gchi-teh sti-ka-las.*"

That spell. The only one she knows. The words that will reveal what she truly is.

26

The effect is monumental and instantaneous. Every bulb and every glass light fitting in the place explodes, spraying shards of glass in all directions, showering both vampires and humans alike. At the same time, the fridge doors blow out, and the glass-topped tables bloom upwards.

"Rey!" Amid the chaos, she is just standing there. Calm. Peaceful, even. At one with the energy of the universe. At least that is how it seems. Then the screaming begins.

Everyone is now on their feet, and the vampires are shrieking and squealing.

"Witch! Witch!"

Any trace of a smile has left the old vampire's face as she stands there, staring at Rey.

"A witch. She's a witch."

Rey's eyes are locked on mine. Somehow, through it all, I can hear her.

"Naz, we need to go! We need to get out of here, *now*!"

I nod, picking myself up, bits of glass falling from my clothes and hair. We'll have to go out the way we came, while the exit is still visible. But it's already too late. The vampires are converging on her.

"Hold her down!"

"Gag her."

"No! No!" I try to reach her again, but I'm pushed back and, within seconds, vamps of all ages and sizes have circled her, growling and snarling like the vicious beasts they are.

"Rey! Rey!"

A hand grabs my shoulder and I see a long, deadly fingernail exposed. For a split second, I think it's going to strike at me but, instead, I'm tossed to the side, as the vamp it's attached to makes its way to my friend.

"Please! Rey!"

My voice is becoming hoarse, as I continue to shout her name while, all around me, the screaming continues as humans, many with deep cuts from the flying glass, run for the exits and more vampires flood into the room. The floor is slick with blood and littered with debris. There's no safe way to move, but I've got to try.

"Get the witch. Hold her down."

"Rey! Rey!"

"Naz!" The sound of her voice causes my heart to leap with hope.

"Rey?" Tears streaming down my cheeks, I try to squeeze through to reach her, but it's no good. With each passing moment, more and more vampires appear, desperate to get hold of the witch, and I'm pushed further and further back.

"Naz! Naz, help me! Please don't leave me, Naz! Please!"

"I'm coming! I'm coming!"

Another hand grabs my shoulder and I move to shake it away, only this time it doesn't push me to the side, but pulls me into a small alcove. When I look up, a gasp leaves my lips.

"Calin?"

"What the hell are you doing here?"

"Please, *please*! We have to get her. We have to save her."

His eyes leave me and turn to the crowd. In the midst of all this chaos, his face is a picture of pure concentration.

"The witch? The witch is your friend?"

"Please, Calin! She only came here for me. You have to … we have too …"

The shouting and screaming continues, only now it's missing something—Rey's voice. She has gone quiet.

"Rey! Rey!" I call out again, gasping through shuddering breaths. But there's no reply. "Calin, you have to do something! You have to!"

He looks across the room again and, for a moment, I think he's going to help her. Then my heart shatters, as he turns back to me and shakes his head.

"There's nothing I can do. I'm sorry."

"Please!" I cling to the front of his jacket and stare up at him.

But his eyes aren't on me. They're looking at someone else now. And that's when I see him – a sight that steals

CHAPTER 26

the very air from my lungs and causes every hair on my body to rise up.

"It's him," I whisper.

"I need to get you out of here," Calin states, grabbing my hands. But my feet don't move.

The pitted skin. The scar above the eyebrow. The face that has haunted my nightmares for a decade is now only feet away from me.

"Narissa!"

"It's him," I repeat. This time Calin pulls me more forcefully, but I dig in my heels and try to resist.

"Look." He shakes me so forcefully that my eyes blur and then refocus.

"This is not safe. I'll do everything I can, but I need you out of here, now. You understand? I will not have your blood on my hands."

I don't know what to say. What about Rey? And what about him? The vampire I have spent so many years of my life searching for. Calin needs to understand. But he doesn't give me a chance to explain. Instead, he scoops me up just as he did the last time he rescued me and races up the staircase and out into the night.

27

I don't know how we're moving so fast, or even where we're going, but I fight with everything I've got against his iron grip, even though I know it's futile and I have no choice but to let him carry me away. If he did put me down, I'd remain wherever he left me, a crumpled, broken heap. I won't be able move on from this. From what I've done, what I've seen. And I think he knows that, too, as he carries me along darkened streets, through parks, over bridges, all the time keeping me pressed tight against his chest, until we're back in Mayfair, back in the flat with the empty fridge and the expensive sheets.

"Here." He hands me a glass, which I lift to my lips without even looking at it. Only when the liquid hits the back of my throat do I realise it's whisky, not water. I go to give it back, before changing my mind and downing the lot.

"That's Macallen Number Six, you're drinking

there," he tells me. "Nearly three-thousand pounds a bottle."

"Then get me something cheaper," I say, placing the glass down on a nearby table.

Without another word, he removes the stopper from the decanter and pours me another measure.

"So, now that you're safe and burning through my whisky, are you going to tell me what you were doing there?" The checked anger in his tone reminds me of Oliver.

Oh my God, what am I going to tell Oliver? Tears instantly fill my eyes, blinding me, as I grope for the glass. I want to down it all again, but the first mouthful catches in my throat and I start to choke. He reaches a hand over to me, but I slap it away and stand up.

"You left her," I spit at him. "You left her there. We need to go back. We have to find her."

"No, we need to keep you safe."

He takes the glass from me and pushes me back onto the sofa.

"What the hell were you playing at, *Narissa*? What were you thinking of, taking a witch into the Blood Bank?"

I snatch the glass back, not sure if I'm going to finish the drink or throw it at him.

Moving over to the cabinet, he fetches another glass, pours one for himself and, lifting it to his lips, takes a long, slow draw.

"I thought vampires couldn't drink anything except blood." There's bitterness in my voice, but I don't care. "And I thought you didn't have anything else in the flat, anyway."

"How about you start by telling me the truth, before judging me? So, Narissa, I assume you work for Blackwatch."

I snort in response. "I told you, it's *Naz*," I say pointedly. "And, as for Blackwatch, I'm not even allowed in the building."

"But you and Grey?"

"Oliver is a friend. My dad worked for Blackwatch." *So did Rey*, I want to add. But I can't even bear to say her name. So instead, I finished my second glass.

"Your father?" Calin asks, tilting his head.

"Michael Knight. Maybe you knew him?"

A single line appears between his eyebrows.

"I did. Well, I knew *of* him. I'm sorry. I heard about his passing. It must have been, what, five years ago now, was it not?"

This time I help myself to more whisky. Of all the people I would have expected to have this conversation with, a vampire was definitely not top of the list. Then again, I didn't expect my best friend to sacrifice herself for me.

His choice of words grates on me. "Ten. And it wasn't *a passing*," I say. "He didn't get ill or die of old age. He was murdered. Murdered by a vampire."

Another line joins the first.

"That's quite an accusation to make, given who your friend works for."

"You think I don't know that? I've spent my entire adult life trying to track him down. And tonight, *tonight*, you dragged me away just as I'd found him! You interfered! And you left her! You left Rey for them to destroy her!"

The memory of her screaming echoes in my head. The screaming—and then the silence. Instinctively, I go to polish off the rest of the drink, but he grabs my hand.

"I'm sorry about your friend," he says. "I … vampires act differently around witches. I know it's not an excuse, but if you knew what they did to us, all those years ago … The way they hunted my kind. Most find it difficult to forgive."

"She did nothing to your kind," I spit at him. "She didn't even know she was a witch until a year ago. And she only knows one, bloody spell. One! How much of a danger could she be to you?"

The combination of the alcohol and the despair suddenly hits me hard and all I want to do is close my eyes. Lifting my legs up onto the sofa, I stifle a yawn.

"Can I sleep here?" My eyes are already starting to close. "Can I stay here? Just for tonight?"

I don't actually see if he nods or shakes his head, but I feel my boots being pulled from my feet and my jacket from around my shoulders. Then a soft blanket is draped carefully over me. *Maybe if I sleep long enough, when I wake up, this will all be over*, I tell myself. I'm a heartbeat away from drifting off, when a low, guttural growl, startles me. Springing upright, I see Calin over by his dining-room table, my jacket in one hand and my crumpled sketch in the other.

"Is this him?" he asks me. "Is this the vampire you're looking for?"

His face is furious, his eyes dark as night and even though his fangs are hidden, I swear I've never seen him look so murderous.

"Yes. That's him. He's the one who murdered my father. Do you know him?"

28

Styx

Humans are to vampires as oysters are to humans—there's no disguising the hideousness of the lesser creatures, no denying their fragility and relative worthlessness. Both contain innards and have a fleshiness that is pretty disgusting and yet, at the right temperature, combined with the appropriate atmosphere and perhaps a glass of fine wine, they become exquisite. Delectable. Divine, even. After all the ones I have tasted, there's something new to be found in every fresh vein. I'm talking, of course, about humans. Not oysters. Oysters are still repulsive.

"Well, that was all very exciting, wasn't it?"

My instinct is to turn around and snarl, but on seeing her there, dressed in all her finery, I catch myself just in time,

"Elizaveta, I didn't realise you were still here."

"Well, I left when you told us to, obviously, but I somehow suspected you wouldn't have gone. You are aware it's past dawn?"

"I'd assumed as much. There were things that needed to be dealt with."

I cast an eye around at the devastation that had previously been our exclusive watering hole.

"Of course," she replies, her smile all-knowing. Hundreds of years she's lived in the city, and nothing goes unnoticed by those hazel eyes of hers. A vampire the likes of Elizaveta is the kind you want fighting on your side. The sort that remembers the old days. As if reading my mind, she brushes out the creases in her skirt and sighs.

"A witch then."

"A witch indeed."

"Well, I never thought I'd see the day again. Certainly not in London. When was the last time we had fun with one of them?"

It's a rhetorical question. She might be three centuries older than I am, but her memory is as sharp as a pin. But I know why she's asking. She wants to reminisce.

"It was Salzburg, as you well know. Outside the Mirabellplatz. 1786. Those three youngsters."

"Of course, but let's not forget the ones that shall not be mentioned." Her eyes twinkle and a coy smile crosses her face.

It's true, there were others that came later. That we killed after signing the Blood Pact with the humans. Yes, we'd enjoyed our sport. A hunt is always stimulating. But those witches … they'd deserved everything they'd had coming to them and more.

"So, do you know anything about her? Where she's come from? Her coven?"

"Nothing as yet. But, in all my time, in all *your* time, have you ever seen anything so reckless? I have to admit, I do find it rather intriguing."

"Intriguing indeed." Breaking a moment from our conversation, Elizaveta bends down to rummage through the piles of broken glass. When she straightens back up, her fingers are wrapped around a delicate, china teacup.

"You have told Polidori and the others, I assume?" she says, blowing gently at the crockery. "They're aware of what happened?"

"I have told Polidori. Beyond that is not my decision."

"And the witch?"

"Again, not my decision. Although there's little to nothing left of her now."

With a groan, I survey the devastation surrounding us. I'll get others to do the clean-up, but it's a job for the night-time. Not for daylight hours.

"I shall let you know when we can reopen," I say, dipping my head in a small bow that is clearly meant as a dismissal. But rather than responding to my subtle message and leaving, she looks at me through narrowed eyes.

"The witch did not come alone, Damien. She had company."

"Company?" I shake my head. "Another like her?"

"Not a witch, a human. A young woman. And she was looking for you."

"A human, looking for me?"

"Yes. Looking for you and carrying this."

From a hidden pocket in her dress, she pulls out a stake. I will confess, I did not see that coming.

"This human, did she say what she wanted?" My eyes are locked on the weapon.

"No," she shakes her head. "She told me that she'd met you before, through a friend, and that you had invited her here. She said she just needed to talk to you, which was obviously a lie. I could smell it on her. There were lots of things I could smell on her, like anger. Rage. Any idea who she could be?"

"A human who is angry at me?" I am forced to chuckle at the comment.

Two hundred years ago, I could have given you dozens of names of those who would have liked to put a stake through my heart for how I had wronged them. But that was in the days before the Blood Pact. Before we had been mutilated by the taking of our lower fangs and forced to agree to being monitored by Blackwatch, with their oppressive adherence to the rules. Then again...

"A woman you say. How old? Early twenties?"

"Yes, I'd say so."

"May I please?" I hold out my hand for the stake, which she willingly surrenders.

Humans think they can distinguish delicate aromas, like the scent of a particular flower or the subtle tannins in a well-aged wine from an oak barrel. But they know nothing. They cannot recognise the subtleties that exist, say, between the different species of the Lavandula genus. They cannot identify the nuances of a freezing winter, or an Indian summer, ripe in the air around them. But I can. And I remember it all.

CHAPTER 28

With the lightest grip, I waft it slowly beneath my nose. She'd let much of herself seep into that wood, and she hadn't even been aware of it. But it's there, all right. The sweat of her palm, the salt within the sweat and the tang of the blood that ran just beneath her skin. Everything is here for me to savour, sweet and musky and ... familiar. Unable to control my reaction, I feel the corners of my lips rising in a smile.

"So, you do know her," she says, reading my expression as only she can.

"Better than that, I know exactly how to find her."

29

Oliver

It's ridiculous how quiet the flat seems without the pair of them. This is what it's meant to be like, after all. My flat. Just me. A single man, in a flat he bought with his hard-earned money. I'm not going to be so crass as to call it a bachelor pad but, I guess it is. I should be pleased to find food still in my fridge when I get home from work, not to mention the fact that the only washing up I have to do is what I've created myself. However, the place feels empty. And it's also hard not to think of both of them when I'm at work, after all Blackwatch is how I met them.

After ruminating on the stillness of the flat, I remove my tie and go to fix myself a protein shake. I should have picked something up from one of the takeaway vans near the office, but by the time I'd left, the queues were full of

4 a.m. drunks, lining up for their fix of deep-fried chicken after a night on the town. Having spent a day and a night sorting out blood donoring schedules, and dealing with one particularly freaked-out, new donor, I'm beat. Poor guy. We do vet them very carefully, making sure that they're tough enough to endure the feeding and smart enough to keep their mouths shut. And, ninety-nine percent of the time, we get it right. But, every now and again, someone slips through the net, either not up to what's asked of them or determined to try and out us to the world. The latter never do, of course. We keep a close eye on the newbies. Any sniff of trouble and a dose of something you definitely can't get over the counter at Boots, in the confines of one of our cell-like 'offices', and they end up not even sure what day of the week it is, let alone what they've just been involved in. It's not the most ethical part of my job, and I don't particularly like it, but it's a case of doing what's needed for the greater good.

This one took a long time to fix, though, and by the time I got home, I was both ravenous and exhausted, unsure whether to eat or sleep first. Hence the protein shake. Life's a compromise.

Switching off the blender, I pour the mixture into a glass, move over to the sofa and switch on the television. A week has passed since I found out about Naz's ridiculous antics. It made sense sending Rey over to keep an eye on her. I feel just a fraction more comfortable knowing she won't try anything too stupid this close to Blackwatch HQ, but to be honest, I want to throttle both of them.

I don't know why I thought Naz had got over her obsession. Why I could possibly have imagined she was finally moving on with her life. All this time that I've worked for Blackwatch, I've never once felt threatened by a vamp. That doesn't mean I don't have a healthy respect for them. I'm not an idiot. But I know they would never let one of their kind ruin all the good work of the Blood Pact. In the same way, we'd never let a rogue donor go running out into the night, screaming about vampires. But what Naz did was different, posing as a donor, meeting a member of the Vampire Council. I wonder if I was just being naive to think I could help her on my own.

And Rey. I know what she wants from me. She's come back for the grimoire pages that we keep stored in the Blackwatch vaults. And there's the smallest part of me that's tempted to give them to her. After all, she did nothing wrong. I should know, I was there with her when Jessop found out. But giving her access to the grimoires would only lead to her having more power, which would in turn put her more at risk from the vampires, if they ever found out.

I've finished my drink and know I need a shower before I go to bed, but I sit a moment longer, mulling over what the hell I should do about my friends. Of course, there's nothing I can do. That's what I've been failing to accept all this time.

Resolute in the knowledge that I really have done all I can for both of them, I go to move, when the phone rings. Instinctively, my jaw clenches. After seventeen hours straight on the job, someone else at Blackwatch can deal with whatever's going wrong now. I'm about to send the call straight to voicemail when a glance at the screen tells me it's not a work number. It's not any number I recognise.

30

Narissa

So many pairs of eyes fill my dreams. My father's, lifeless and open as he lies on the cold ground. Rey's, tear-filled and pleading, before they're lost in a sea of vampires. Even my mother's, deep amber and full of a pain I can't fathom. All of them staring at me, accusing me of failure.

I'm still in one of these nightmares, tossing at turning, when two voices start to dominate it, demanding attention. Voices which don't make any sense together. They're becoming louder and seem not to be just inside my head any more but outside it, too. That's when I realise. They're not part of my dream.

"Oliver?" I feel a crick in my neck, as I sit up and see him standing in the kitchen area. When he sees me awake, he takes a step towards me, then stops and shakes his head.

"Tell me this isn't true, Naz. Please, tell me it's not true."

I am not even on my feet, when the tears start to stream down my face.

"She thought it would be okay. I told her to go. I told her to leave. To wait for me outside."

"Why?" He continues to shake his head, as Calin steps back, giving us room for our grief and anger. Although, I'm not sure it's possible to give that kind of space.

"She was trying to help me. To help me find him."

And, like that, Oliver's face changes from white to red.

"This has to stop, Narissa!" he yells. "This obsession! They'll have killed her! *You* have killed her, Narissa! You've killed our best friend!"

"I know." Hot tears tumble down my cheeks. I close my eyes, but her face flashes in front of me. Her eyes, wide with fear. "I … I …"

His gaze bores into me.

"Please, please let this be enough. This has got to be enough for you to stop doing this."

I see the pain in his eyes. Hear the tremble in his voice. And I want to give him the answer he wants to hear. I really do. But today, more than ever, I can't.

"I found him, Oliver, I found him."

"What?" Anger and sadness momentarily give way to surprise.

"It's true. I saw him there, at the end. I even know his

name. He's real. Tell him, Calin. Tell him you know him."

For the first time since I've woken, Oliver's attention shifts from me to Calin.

"Is this true?"

Calin nods, stepping back into the conversation. "From what Narissa has told me, I believe I know the vampire she's described. And I believe what she says happened, too. If anyone would risk breaking the Blood Pact, it would be him."

The colour drains further from Oliver's face.

"Do you have any evidence?"

"Only Narissa's word and I'm afraid that won't be enough. Besides, it's more complicated than that. If I'm right, he's a member of the Council."

"Oh shit."

"I need time to figure out how we can proceed. I will speak to the Head of the Council—"

"Polidori is—"

"—is an old and trusted friend. But it needs to be done delicately. I can't simply march in, casting aspersions about another vampire, especially a Council member."

Scepticism is written all over Oliver's face.

"Why would you do this? Why would you go against another member?"

This is met with a stony glare.

"Why do you think? I believe in the Blood Pact. I believe in what we have accomplished. For someone like Damien Styx to think he can undo all that, is not acceptable."

"Styx?"

"Yes, I expect you've seen him on your donor rota quite a lot. Masquerades as one of the gentry. Believe me, he is anything but. Also …" He pauses. "I do feel at least a little responsible for what has happened. Had I been quicker to realise that Narissa was not one of your regulated donors, I would have alerted you and we may never have reached this situation."

"Well, you're right about that, at least."

I've never seen Oliver be so cold with anyone. If I had to guess which of them might try ripping out the other's throat first, my money would not be on Calin. I think he sees that too.

"At least there's no need to think he'd be after Naz, after all this time. I mean, how would he even know she's been looking for him?"

At this point, I look at the ground. I've already told Calin about the woman with the tea cup. She's some old, Russian, aristocrat apparently and close to Styx. He may not have known I was after him before, but I'm betting he does now. Thankfully, Calin doesn't go into the details.

"He'll know. What we need to do now is make sure Narissa is kept safe. I will find out what I can about him, see if there's some tangible way we can link him to agent Knight's death although, like I said, I will need to tread carefully. If I go in gung-ho, it's likely to end poorly.'

"So, what are you suggesting?" Oliver asks.

"She can't be out at night. Not ever. And I think it would be better if she isn't left alone then, either. Can you change your shifts, so you're only working days? I can put in a call to Blackwatch myself, if that would make it easier for you."

"Thank you, but I'm perfectly capable of arranging my own schedule."

"Of course. What about accommodation? Do you have room for Narissa to stay with you? If you prefer, the pair of you could stay here. Or I have another place, in Kensington?"

"Of course you do," Oliver mutters. "We'll be fine at mine."

With that, their conversation appears to be at an end, and Oliver picks up his coat, before turning to me.

"Get your things," he says, like I'm some child he's reprimanding for misbehaving at school.

My whole body shrinks inwards. Instinctively, my eyes go to Calin. I'm not sure what I'm expecting him to say or do, but when he meets my gaze, he simply nods. Then, turning back to Oliver, he takes out his phone.

"I'll be in touch," he says.

31

Calin

I am at a loss what to do. All day I have paced this flat, forgoing sleep to try and come up with some sort of plan. Some way of honouring my promise to bring Styx to justice. She's telling the truth, of that there's no doubt. The certainty in her voice. The strength of her heartbeat. There was not a single trace of mendacity, although I know that the human memory can play tricks, and I myself have seen how pain and grief can so easily distort events.

I recall things from my human days, so clearly that I will never forget. During the war, I clung to memories of home—all I had to keep me going. Then there are the pictures in my head of the atrocities I had to witness during that period, that no amount of trying will obliterate.

CHAPTER 31

The problem is that, no matter how great my memory is, my mind is still as empty as it was when the pair of humans first left. If anything, it's even more devoid of ideas. At least then I was hopeful. Cautious but still optimistic that I could find a way to bring agent Knight the justice he deserved. Narissa too. Now, I am not so sure what I can do. I just know I have to try.

My phone buzzes and draws my attention away from the problem.

Gathering. Thirty minutes.

There's no need for any more details.

Messages have been coming through all day. Gossip mongering, scavenging for further news about the witch. But they shan't get any from me.

A hundred times, I have cursed the situation I've found myself in. What I said to Oliver was true. From that first meeting with Narissa, I knew that something was different about her. Something didn't make sense— the way she surveyed me and the way she failed to question my existence. But I was too intrigued to do the right thing, to contact Blackwatch. And now this has happened. I cannot concern myself with the witch just yet. Not until I have dealt with Styx.

By the time I am ready to leave, I have the most rudimentary of plans. One that sickens me to the very core. It's a long shot, of course, but what I need is evidence, and it's like searching for a needle in a haystack, when you're not even sure there's a needle to be found. Styx has been doing this a long time. Longer than me. Far smarter and wiser vampires than him have fallen prey to witches and other hunters throughout the years. He has survived by his instincts and through deception. All I can hope is that his ego is fragile enough that I can poke it and get a reaction. But to do that, I have to spend time with him. Befriend him, even. Vampires don't get drunk easily, but it does happen. And I suspect when I tell him the value of my whisky collection, he will take great satisfaction in trying to deplete it, and maybe that will loosen his tongue.

Colder nights are upon us now. As I step out onto the street, I cast a quick glance at the moon, partially hidden by clouds but still gleaming brightly. Polidori has assured us the meeting will be a swift affair, but we have important matters to discuss. By 9 p.m. we are all gathered. All except for one. There's little conversation between members of the Council before a session. Some of us are friends, but mostly we are colleagues, if you can call it that. All but two members are glued to the screens of their phones. These ancient beings are just as much slaves to technology as mere mortals are.

"Right, if we can take our seats." Polidori calls the meeting to order. "I think we all know what we're here to discuss."

"Should we not wait for Styx?" I ask, acutely aware of the empty seat opposite me.

"Damien is clearing up the remainder of the mess at the Blood Bank. I assume you have all heard about the attack by the witch last night."

Murmurs of agreement rise up around me.

"What about the witch?"

It was a question I had been going to ask, although having one of the others beat me to it is much better.

"Yes." Polidori lets out a long sigh. "It's unfortunate.

Most unfortunate. She didn't survive. I realise that the death of a human, any human, at our hands cannot be tolerated. However, in this situation, those present acted out of fear and in self-defence. Any jury, human or vampire, would understand that."

"So, the humans have been told?" I hear my voice, before I even realise I was going to speak. "You have told Blackwatch of the incident?"

"Naturally, they were informed."

"And the Blood Pact?" asks another member of the Council.

"The Blood Pact is intact. Blackwatch agreed with us. This was an unprovoked attack. All we can hope to do now is put this terrible incident behind us."

More murmurs, more sad looks. Yes, the attack was unprovoked, to a degree, but how many vampires does it take to bring down one, inexperienced witch? Venom could have sedated her.

"Calin, is everything okay?" Polidori looks at me, enquiringly.

There's only one answer I can give. But, for the first time in nearly a hundred years, I feel my sire is hiding something from me. His grey eyes shimmer as they hold my gaze.

"Yes," I say, offering my most agreeable smile. "It's fine, Sir. Everything's completely fine."

32

Narissa

It's been three days. Three days stuck in Oliver's flat, with Oliver. He can't even look me in the eye. I've tried to speak to him, tried to apologise, but he won't hear it.

The first day, he slept until gone noon, then stayed in his room, only coming out to use the bathroom and not even acknowledging me when he did. When I cooked a meal, eggs on toast, he said he wasn't hungry. Half an hour later, a takeaway appeared at the door. I guess it was just my company he didn't have any appetite for. I can't say I blame him.

The second day, he went to work as usual, returning home at dusk. Most of the time he was in his room, taking endless phone calls. When he wasn't, he was answering messages and trying his hardest not to look at me. I get it. I can't even look at myself. I can't look in a mirror without seeing her. Without hearing her voice in my head. How can I have screwed up so badly?

Today, I've decided to leave the flat. I just have to get out. I'll go insane otherwise. I'm not planning on being out long. Just a few hours. Just to get a little space. I'll be back by sunset, which is all Oliver really cares about. Just so long as I'm not out after dark, screwing up more things in the vampire world, he'll carry on ignoring me.

It isn't until I step outside that I realise what an amazing day it is. The sky's a bright cerulean and there's barely a cloud. I love that word. Cerulean. Like blue just isn't good enough for a day like this. And it's true, it's not. Walking along the South Bank, I stop and gaze out over the water. If it wasn't for the tourist boats going up and down, it would be almost motionless. And that's when it hits me. I really am all alone.

"I'm sorry," I say, staring at the soft ripples below me. "I'm so sorry, Dad. I got it all wrong. I just … I needed them to know what happened. But I messed up. And now I've got no one. What am I meant to do? I want to put it all right. I need someone to tell me what to do. Tell me how to fix everything."

I wait, like maybe the answer will rise up out of the water, or fall down from the sky, or maybe, just maybe, I'll turn towards the street and see him there, walking towards me. But there's nothing. Nothing but an endless sea of strangers.

Back at the house, Oliver is already home and less than pleased to see me, as usual.

"What the hell are you playing at?" he demands, the

moment I step through the door. "Do you have any idea how worried you've had me?"

"I went for a walk."

"I've been trying to get hold of you for the last hour."

"You have?" I reach in my pocket and pull out my phone, only to find the battery's flat. "Sorry, I didn't realise."

"You didn't realise. You know I'm busting a gut here, trying to keep you safe."

"I don't need *keeping safe*. I was out in daylight hours. No vamps are going to come out then."

"You don't know that. You don't know what they might do."

His mood is even worse than usual. With no bedroom to lock myself away in, I head for the bathroom instead.

"Is it okay if I run myself a bath?"

"Do what you like. That's what you normally do, isn't it?"

I stiffen at this snide remark. Biting down, I force myself to ignore it and walk away. I'm almost there, but I can still feel his eyes boring into the back of my head. All that judgement. All that self-righteousness. And I've had enough.

"You know I never asked her to take me," I say, spinning round and finding myself just a few feet away from Oliver's now-permanent scowl. "I didn't even know the place existed. She chose to tell me about it. *She* took *me*."

"And you just let her, knowing the risk."

"No, I didn't! And I tried to make her leave. I thought she *had* left."

"That's not good enough."

"What? What would you have had me do? Push her out the door?"

"Yes, that's exactly what you should have done. She should never have been anywhere near the vampires. You know that. You should have been looking out for her."

"She was a grown woman, Oliver!"

And just like that, it hits me like a baseball to the gut —I've used the past tense. When I next speak, my voice comes out weak, trembling. "Do you honestly believe I would ever have intentionally done anything that would put her in harm's way? Do you really believe I thought this might happen?"

"I don't think you thought at all," he replies coldly. "I don't think you consider anyone but yourself."

"That's not fair."

"Isn't it? Stealing from Joe? The unauthorised blood donoring? Getting mixed up with Calin? How much more are you going to screw up, Naz? How many more lives are you going to ruin, before you finally realise that the whole fucking world doesn't revolve around you?"

Every fibre of my being fizzes with anger. I want to stand up to him. Want to argue back. But I know he's right, and it's actually myself that I'm mad at.

"When this is all over," he says, "we're through. I'll give the vampire however long he thinks it'll take. A month. Two. Whatever. But when *it's* done, *we're* done. Not friends, not acquaintances. Nothing. When we've got this Styx, you and I are over. I want you out of my life for good."

"Oliver ..." Tears escape down my cheeks.

"I'm done with it, Naz. You're toxic. This is over."

It's worse than a physical pain. Worse than Joe trying

to beat the life out of me in a dark alley. Never before have words affected me so keenly. It feels like my heart has been ripped apart. And there's nothing more left to say. No excuses I can offer. He's right. I ruin everything.

"As soon as this is done," I finally manage, "you never have to see me again."

33

Styx

The last two centuries have seen changes that we could never have anticipated. And not all for the better. I will agree there are some advantages to the Blood Pact. I'm not going to lie, I enjoy not being hunted anymore. Not being jolted awake, to find my nest alight through the nefarious actions of some witch, intent on my demise. I enjoy the option of being able to stay put somewhere. Being able to reside in one town, one house even, for a few years or decades or even centuries, without the need to move on if someone grows suspicious. And sanitation is far better nowadays too. It would also be remiss of me to discount other beneficial developments of the nineteen and twentieth centuries. Education. Transportation. Technology. Thanks to the freedom to roam the human world, both real and virtual, I know infinitely more about it than I could previously have thought possible, and for that I am also grateful.

But there are things I miss. The thrill as you stalk your prey down a dark alley, on a moonless night. Smog filling the streets, as you slide through the shadows. The choice: go all the way and leave them lifeless on the ground; or just take a sip, a mere taste, a fleeting bite so brief, they barely even notice. Leave them wondering if they are seeing and hearing things. The creation of insanity—that is something I used to really enjoy.

However, the problem, as I see it, is that not only did the way we live and feed change, it's we ourselves who are different.

Before the arrival of the Blood Pact, we were free to sire whomever we liked, whenever we liked. If I were yearning for the company of, say, a pianist, I could find myself one and turn him, so that I could enjoy his talent day or night, without having to pander to such human foibles as tiredness or hunger. Then, when a year or so had passed and I'd found my tastes had moved on to, say, the cello, I could drive a stake through his heart and select a new playmate.

Now, no humans are allowed to be sired without the agreement of the Council. No one can be turned simply for the fun of it. They must meet criteria. Be exceptional. What does that mean? Well, it means the vampire world is becoming full of self-righteous elitists. Leaders of industry, who play at being philanthropists and desire to continue giving long after their mortal shell would have worn out. Smarmy politicians, who have greased the wheels somewhere along the line. Occasionally, a little nepotism creeps in as well. Yes, Calin Sheridan, I'm talking about you. There are no working-class vampires like there used to be. None who pulled themselves up by their boot straps, as they struggled to survive rat-invested streets, stealing loaves of bread and picking pockets, just so they could survive.

That was me. Born into poverty, I learned to steal decades before I learned to read and write. And, no matter what education I have acquired, no matter what company I may now choose to keep, there's still that part of me that delights in the skill of being able to slip a hand into a fellow's breast pocket, literally right under his nose, without him even noticing.

The fallout from the Blood Bank incident took three days to deal with. Finding workmen who can keep their mouths shut hasn't always been easy, but we do now have people on our books who we can trust to be discrete. As I oversaw the work, I toyed with the stake Elizaveta had taken from the girl, breathing in its scent again and getting more and more excited about what was to come. A proper hunt. Well almost. More a cunning trap.

"Styx," says Calin, by way of a greeting when I arrive outside the chamber.

His smug face is enough to make me want to stake him right there and then. Not that I suspect he even realises how he looks. Some men are just born with a self-satisfied smugness plastered all over their faces. Still, this is probably the first greeting he's volunteered in over sixty years. Funny that. Beneath his outward indifference, I cannot help but notice a hint of exhaustion in his features. His shoulders are ever-so-slightly slumped, his eyes ever-so-slightly dulled. I'm obviously not the only one who has been busy. But now it's time for me to focus on finding the girl. The first step of my plan is already in place. The second will involve golden boy here.

"Sheridan." I try to keep my voice neutral, despite the fact that every fibre of my being wants to slip the stake from my pocket and drive it into his boy-scout heart.

"I hear you did a great job getting the Blood Bank fixed up. Thank you."

And now a compliment too. Interesting. Perhaps he knows about the link between myself and the girl. That could pose a problem but, then again, it could make it all the more fun.

"Thank you. And I'm sorry about the Scotland situation. That must be irritating. Are you quite sure you managed to stake them properly?"

"Scotland situation?"

"Have you not heard? Oh, I'm sorry. I'm sure Polidori will update us all. We should get seated. We don't want to keep the others waiting."

There is an obscene amount of gratification to be gained from watching someone you thoroughly dislike squirm in discomfort. It may well be my third favourite activity. After drinking blood and killing, that is.

As we take our seats, I ensure my smile stays firmly in place and mostly aim it at Calin.

"Thank you all," Polidori says, as well fall silent. "We have a few items on the agenda."

He works his way through a list of mundane housekeeping tasks, before finally arriving at what I've been waiting for.

"The situation up in Scotland. It would appear that it isn't quite as resolved as we'd thought."

"In what way?" Calin asks. "I found the rogue. I can assure you they are disposed of."

"Yes, well, there has been another death. My guess is that he had sired another, before you got to him."

Across the table, Calin shakes his head, and my satisfaction increases. Seeing him sweat over a possible mess up; I could watch this all day.

"I feel that's unlikely. She was young. I find it difficult to believe she would have known the intricacies."

"In any case, it needs dealing with," says Polidori.

"Perhaps," I suggest, eager to stir the pot, "the area needs monitoring over a longer period of time, to really get to the bottom of it."

"Yes, Damien, I think that would be a prudent move."

"Would you like me to go? It will obviously take me a bit of time to get the lie of the land, but it shouldn't take too long," I offer.

Just as I knew he would, Polidori takes a moment to digest my words.

"There's no point someone new wasting time going over old ground. Calin, you will go back and rectify the situation. I'll have a car made available as soon as we finish. The quicker we can get this dealt with, the better."

"Of course," answers Sheridan. "I will just need to make a few arrangements before I leave."

"Go and make them right away. I'll tell the driver to be ready."

As he rises to leave the room, it's hard not to grin. But there will be time to pat myself on the back later. Just one more job to finish off.

Moments later, Polidori dismisses the rest of us. I

move swiftly and, fortunately, Calin is still in the corridor, typing away on his phone.

"Letting the butler know of your departure?" In my defence, I do know I sound like a prick.

"Something like that."

He finishes the message and slips the phone into his back pocket.

"Well," I say, draping my arm across his shoulder, "as I mentioned before, if you need any help up there, I'm more than happy."

His discomfort is obvious. He is clearly unhappy with this uncharacteristic familiarity. The very act of me touching him is probably enough to make his skin crawl —and, to be fair, it's entirely mutual but also necessary, so I push on.

"I'll be sure to remember that," he says, slipping himself free. And with that, he turns around and walks to the door. I wait until he's out of sight and then weigh the phone in the palm of my hand. I doubt he will notice the switch for quite a while.

Once a pickpocket, always a pickpocket.

34

Narissa

We didn't speak again after the row last night, when he told me he wanted me out of his life for good. I get it. I understand. I'm not going to deny that part of me hopes after he's slept on it he'll reconsider, but Oliver never says anything he doesn't mean. It's one of the things I used to love the most about him.

I'm already awake and reading, when I see his bedroom door open. I hurriedly hide the book under the duvet and close my eyes, pretending to be asleep. I hear his footsteps stop by the edge of the sofa and can almost feel his shadow hanging over me, but he stays silent. He moves to the kitchen, then to the bathroom, and all the while I keep my eyes closed, wondering if this is what it's like being in one of those marriages you always hear about, where the husband and wife secretly despise each other, but stay together for the kids, or the money, or whatever. I'm not sure if our reason is more or less complicated—tracking down a murderous vampire, without destroying a two-hundred-year-old truce in the process.

I haven't heard from Calin. Not even a short text to check I'm still standing, but I'm fairly sure he's in contact with Oliver. In all the time I've known him, his phone has never buzzed half as many times as it has these last couple of days. Once, I would have sneaked a look at it, just to confirm my suspicions, but not now. I've done enough. More than enough.

When the front door closes, I open my eyes and stretch out. I should have three lectures today—four-and-a-half hours of listening to people analysing books I read years ago. Surprisingly, the prospect actually fills me with some cheer. Oliver might want to keep me prisoner, but he knows as well as I do that I'm perfectly safe during daylight hours and, even if Styx was trying to track me down, a lecture hall filled with three-dozen English students, is hardly the ideal location for an attack.

So, sticking to main roads and well-lit areas, I enjoy my first bit of normality in what feels like months. On the way, I buy Wendy a bacon sandwich and give Jeff a pat, almost like a normal day. Between lectures, I sit in the student café and look like any other undergrad, phone in hand, willing it to do something.

It isn't until I get back to Oliver's that a message comes through. Calin. *Can I see you tonight? At 6?* At least he knows I still exist. I hadn't realised quite how much I've missed him. Well, not him per se. I don't know him well enough to be sure if I could even like him, but his presence. The way he let me talk that night, after pulling me out of the Blood Bank. The way he didn't doubt that I was telling the truth, not even for a moment. So, seeing this message, I know straight away what my answer will be.

I'll be there in an hour, I reply.

Just time to shower and eat. And I'd better leave Oliver a note, given his reaction last night at finding me missing from the flat. The shower and food part are easy. The note, not so much. *Gone to Calin's,* I write at the top, then struggle to figure out what comes next. Back later? I'll call you? He'll have a fit if I walk back on my own, but he'd most likely have one if I stay at Calin's too so, instead, I just leave it at that.

As I walk down the stairs and out onto the street, my mind is racing. Is Calin expecting to feed from me? I wonder instinctively. It doesn't seem likely. After all, now he knows I'm not with Blackwatch and especially in the current climate, he's unlikely to want to break the rules. Which means it can only be about my father. About Styx. Maybe he's invited Oliver to join us, too. A large part of me hopes that's not the case. I could do with a few more hours without more judgement being heaped on me.

I reach Mayfair and I'm ready for any possibility. Maybe he's already got Styx. Or maybe he's going to tell me it's impossible to bring my father's killer to justice.

I take the lift to the third floor. The iron grille rattles open and I turn into the corridor, towards Calin's apartment, then freeze as I see the figure waiting there. The pitted face breaks into a smile. The eyes are narrow and even darker than I remember, but there's no mistaking that scar. That sneer. That murderous look.

"Perfect timing," he says, running his fingers over the keypad beside the door. "Perhaps you'd be so kind as to let us in."

35

I throw myself back between the closing lift doors, but he's too fast. He blocks them from sliding shut and drags me out.

"No!" I scream, as the doors shut and my escape route is lost. My eyes flicker towards the stairwell.

"You make one more move and it will be your last," he says. "Now, I can do the job here, leave you on the carpet for your boyfriend or the butler to find, or we can go inside and talk about this like civilised people."

"He's not my boyfriend," I spit at him.

He cocks his head to the side. "Really? That's what you took from my last sentence?"

"And you're not a person, you're a monster," I snarl.

"Well, that I would have to agree with," he says, pulling me along the corridor. "Now, open the door."

"Why?"

"Why? Did I not make myself clear? I will snap your neck, little girl. I will rip your heart from your chest."

"You'll do the same in there."

He smiles. "I'd like to say that maybe you're not as stupid as I first thought, but there's still plenty of evidence to the contrary."

He grabs the handle and twists it all the way around, until the lock pops.

"What do you know? I guess I didn't need your help after all. Now get inside."

My instinct is still to try and run for it, but I know there's no way I'd be fast enough. Still, I'm not going to just walk in there. Not a chance.

He leans towards me.

"There's an old man in the apartment below." His voice a low hiss. "With an irregular heartbeat. Possibly angina, but probably more serious. A little dose of venom from my nail wouldn't likely be very helpful. Upstairs, there's a couple. They're cooking dinner. I expect they have an expensive set of chef's knives. Cooking can be stressful, you know. Arguments can break out. Maybe he'll get so angry that he'll throw a knife and accidentally strike her in the chest. Then, he'll probably be so wracked with guilt that he'll throw himself out their fourth-floor bedroom window. You never know what the consequences might be if you don't get inside the flat, *now*."

I'm not stupid enough to resist any more.

"Okay," I whisper and take a step, despite the shaking fit that's almost overwhelming me. "I'll come."

As I step into the flat, I scan the room. Everything is in its place. Everything neatly arranged, without so much as a cushion awry. But it feels wrong. Not really surprising, given the company.

"If you're looking for your boyfriend, I'm afraid he's

preoccupied." Styx's voice is back to normal now, but even normal is terrifying.

He kicks the door shut with his heel, only to be slouched on the sofa a millisecond later.

"He has lots of important business to deal with. He's probably going to be gone for the next few days. And, unfortunately, there seems to have been a bit of a mix up with his phone." His smile reveals his fangs, as he reaches into his pocket and pulls out what I presume to be the device in question. "Now, you and I have got plenty to talk about, haven't we? We've met before, of course. I will admit, it took me a little while to work out who could be so intent on finding me. And bringing a witch with you, too. That really was a bonus. I should probably let you live, just for that."

I think I might puke at any minute.

"What did you do to her?"

He lifts his hands, as if pleading innocence.

"Me? Oh no. It was all over by the time I stepped in. Which is such a shame. I hear she was delicious. There's something about the blood of a witch, you know, something, well, magical."

As he lounges on the sofa, I edge closer to the kitchen area, thinking of all those knives, laid out neatly in the drawer there. As if they'd be of any actual use. If only I could use my phone. Ring Oliver. But then what? Even if I managed to dial, which I wouldn't, Styx could kill me before Oliver had even grabbed his coat.

"Does he keep anything to drink here?" he asks, suddenly on his feet and opening one cabinet after another. "Did you know vampires can get drunk, by the way? It's not easy, but it does help to forget some of the terrible things we've done. If you think of them as terrible. Which I suspect your boyfriend does. From what I hear, he's never really appreciated the beauty of what we are. I don't know how he's deserved his position on the Council. Maybe it's for his love of humans."

His eyes move from the cabinets back to me.

"I could smell you on him, you know. I could smell your blood on his breath. He must have taken a fair bit for it to be so strong. Did he go too far? You can tell me. You know I'm very good at keeping secrets."

He's about to continue, when he's interrupted by the ringing of the house phone beside him. Lifting the device to his ear, he keeps his gaze on me.

"Well, what do you know? Calin, how nice of you to call. There seems to have been a bit of a mix up. Hang on. What was that? You're not very clear at the moment. Wait a second. Just let me put you on speaker phone."

He presses a button and Calin's voice breaks into the room.

"If you harm a hair on her head—"

"Calin!" I scream, lunging for the phone, as if it might somehow be able to save me, although Styx snatches it away before I can get anywhere near.

"I'm sorry, Narissa. I'm sorry. I didn't—"

"Yes, yes, this is all very emotional and touching, but I'm afraid we have other things to be getting on with."

He holds the phone above his head, taunting me, as Calin's voice continues down the line.

"I will hunt you down, Styx. I swear, if you hurt her in any way—"

With a squeeze of his hand, the phone is reduced to a twisted mass of plastic and metal.

"Well, that was entertaining, wasn't it? Unfortunately, I believe he's all the way up in Scotland right now. Even sprinting, a vampire is going to take some time to cover that sort of distance. Now, remind me, where were we?"

His eyes glint with enjoyment. It's all a game to him, of course, but sooner or later, I'm going to end up dead. From the evil sneer on his face, I'm thinking that sooner would be the better option. But there's one question I need answering first. The one I said I would risk dying to find the answer to. And he's the only one who can tell me.

"Why?" I demand, finally stepping forwards. "Why my dad. Of all the people in the world, why did you have to choose him? What did he do to you?"

"Do?" He contemplates the question. "What could he possibly have done to me? I'm sorry if you've been searching for some great revelation, some great conspiracy to expose, but I'm afraid there is none. I fancied killing someone, so I went out that night and snapped a man's neck. That's it."

"That's not true."

"No?"

"You're telling me, of all the people in London, you randomly chose a member of Blackwatch?"

"Your father was in Blackwatch?" His eyes widen, in what is meant to be surprise. "Well, isn't that a coincidence. I had no idea," he says, but I can read liars, vampire or not. He's hiding the truth.

"Did he find out what you do in your spare time?" I ask, taking another step towards him. "Or did you kill him out of jealousy? Maybe you've never known what it's like to be loved, like he was. Maybe it was as simple as that."

"Oh you silly, naive, little girl."

I step towards him again. There's no fear now, just certainty. I am going to die tonight, here, in this room, staring into the eyes that have haunted me for a decade. There's nothing left to be afraid of.

"You can tell me the truth," I say, so close to him that I can see the points of his fangs. See the dark abyss of his pupils. "We know it will never leave this room. I deserve the truth, at least. Tell me. Why did you kill him?"

He steps closer and raises a hand. His ice-cold fingers caress the side of my neck and I stifle a gasp. A stray tear weaves its way down my cheek.

"As you wish."

I hold my breath, waiting for the last words I will ever hear.

The crash of the door, as it slams open, startles us both and our heads snap in unison towards the sound.

"Get away from her, *now*!"

36

He stands in the doorway, his customised Glock trained on Styx.

"Oliver?"

The combination of relief and panic is somehow preventing me from making sense of what I'm seeing. Not that it matters. The peace I'd felt only moments before, resigned to dying, has evaporated. I don't want to die. I want to live. I really want to live.

"Oliver!" I shout, but he doesn't even acknowledge me.

"Damien Styx, you are to be handed over to the Vampire Council for the murder of Michael Knight."

His face is as hard as stone, his eyes unblinking and, for a split second, fear seems to flash across Styx's face. Then it's gone. He throws back his head and laughs.

"You know I *am* the Vampire Council?"

"Not any more. Blackwatch have been informed, an extermination crew will be here in minutes. It's over."

While they remained focused on each another, I

retreat to Oliver's side. "They're all coming," he says in a whisper, still not breaking eye contact with Styx, and something in my heart feels fit to burst.

Styx raises his hands with a shrug and a smile.

"How did you know?" I ask, tears now blurring my eyes.

"Calin and I have been in daily contact. When I saw your note, I knew there was no way he would have arranged something without running it past me."

In daily contact with Calin? In normal circumstances, that's something I would dwell on, but this is not normal.

"Thank you," I say, standing straighter. "Thank you for coming for me."

This almost feels like forgiveness, but I'm well aware I've got a long way to go before we reach that point. At least he hasn't left me to die. A split second later, laughter fills the room again, harsh and rasping, like nails on a blackboard.

"You're thanking him? For what? You'll both be dead in a moment."

"Blackwatch are on their way. Jessop will be informing the Vampire Council as we speak."

"Is that so? Well, I can't hear any screeching tyres, or men running outside, so I guess I've got a few minutes left yet, haven't I?"

I barely see him coming, as Styx leaps through the air, but Oliver is ready. The thump-hiss tells me he's got a shot off, as he ducks to the side, but it's not enough to slow him down. He lands soundlessly behind Oliver and, in an instant, he has his arms coiled around his neck.

"No!" I scream, kicking at him. It's not the best kick in the world, not by a long shot, but it catches him by surprise and gives Oliver the chance to slip out of his grip and pull a menacing-looking stake from inside his jacket. The whole scene in front of me is a blur. Styx strikes at him, again and again and again, but Oliver somehow manages to keep blocking him. That's his ploy, I realise. He's not trying to strike Styx, not trying to kill him. He's just wants to keep the fight going long enough for help to arrive. Dodging out of the way, I run to the window and pull up the sash.

"Help!" I scream out into the night. "Help! We're up here! Help us!"

I can't see any movement down below, but I just have to trust they'll be here soon. Fourteen minutes, that's how long it's supposed to take an ambulance, isn't it? And surely Blackwatch would be faster than that. Five minutes, I tell myself. Oliver just needs to hold on for another few minutes. But it's looking less and less likely with every punch. While Styx bounds from sofa to table, Oliver is tiring. Styx lands a punch straight to the jaw. Oliver wobbles, then rights himself, only to take another blow.

"No!" I yell, rushing towards them, but I'm not fast enough.

Grabbing him with both hands, Styx picks him up and throws him at the wall.

"Oliver!"

Plaster comes crumbling down around him, as he folds forwards onto the ground.

"No!" I lunge at Styx, only to have him throw me back with barely a flick of his arm.

"I've had enough of this," he snarls. "Time to be done with the pair of you."

"Oliver! Oliver, please!"

He groans, blood trickling from the corner of his mouth. He's still alive, but for how long?

As if reading my thoughts, Styx steps forwards and wraps an arm around my neck.

"I'm going to make you watch me kill him first," he hisses in my ear. "After all, we still have a little bit of time left to enjoy this. No one seems to have arrived yet."

I feel the pad of a fingertip trace a line down from my ear to my collar bone. I can't see that dagger-like nail, which must be poised and ready.

"Did you know that, with the right amount of venom in your system, you can still be awake, yet paralysed? Did your boyfriend tell you that? Did he tell you all the ways we can enjoy ourselves?"

Every part of me wants to kick and scream, but I know there's no point and I know that's what he wants and I'm damn well not going to give him the satisfaction. So I stay silent and let him continue with his monologue.

"We could have had so much fun together, you and I," he says. "Don't you think?"

"Go to hell," I spit back.

His laughter rattles in my ear. "Oh, darling, I've been there so many times already. Now, where were we?"

This time, it's the hard edge of his nail I feel. Still no point though, just pressure against my skin. I hold my breath, waiting for the pain of the cut.

"Maybe I would have turned you, in the old days. I could have shown you how beautiful this life can be."

"I'd rather die."

He sniffs. "Well, yes, that is the obvious alternative.

For now, I'm just going to make you watch, as I drain your friend dry."

"Blackwatch are on their way. They'll be here any minute."

"Ah yes, a minute. You'd be amazed at how much I can achieve in such a short period of time. Now, this won't hurt a bit."

The tip of his nail pieces my skin. The pain is instant. All consuming … and then gone.

The world slips away.

37

The pain comes instantly and everywhere.

I don't understand. What's going on, Oliver? Oliver? I scream, but my voice makes no sound. My vision's changing. Sharpening. Strengthening. *Hang on,* I try to tell him. *Please hang on.*

A noise comes from somewhere behind me. It's a cross between a hiss and a snarl. I feel it's meant to convey strength, or maybe defiance, but all I can smell is fear.

I turn, and there is Styx, cowering. Cowering from me, I suddenly realise—there's no one else here. He bares his fangs, but I bare mine and I launch at him, clawing at his chest and biting into his throat.

Then nothing. Nothing but darkness.

38

When I open my eyes, it's the cold that strikes me first, so sudden, so violent that I think for a moment I've been plunged into icy water. I find I'm actually lying naked on a freezing, stone floor, perfectly dry, although my skin is covered in goose bumps. There's the echo of pain in my bones, like they've been broken and reformed a thousand times over. Images of blood and torn flesh linger in the periphery of my memory, but I can't make any sense of them.

Blinking, I try to adjust to the light, only there isn't any. Not really. Just a small glimmer, coming from a narrow window with metal crosspieces high up in one of the walls. If I didn't feel bad enough already, this isn't helping. Gradually turning onto all fours, I grope around and my hands find more metal. Metal bars.

"Hello?" I call out into the darkness, and the sound of my voice echoes back to me. Wherever this is, it's big. "Where am I? Can anyone hear me? Why am I here?"

I manage to stand and start to explore further. More

metal bars and then what seems to be a metal door, padlocked shut.

"My name is Narissa Knight. Can someone please tell me what I'm doing here? Please? My name is Narissa Knight." I jump back, as my foot lands on something soft and sticky. As I strain to see in the near darkness, I make out a large lump of flesh, flies buzzing around it, "Urgh!" I cover my mouth, gagging, before stepping to the side and hammering on the door.

"Please, my name is Narissa Knight. I'm a student. I live in Tower Hamlets. I'm twenty-four years old."

This is what you're meant to do when you've been kidnapped, isn't I? Reel off fact after fact, so your kidnapper is forced to accept you're a real person. My brain searches for more.

"I'm studying English literature. I worked in the West End, at Joe's Bar—"

I stop, as a silhouette appears in the shadows in front of me. An image that gets clearer as it gets nearer. I instinctively step back. It's a vampire, I realise. The way it moves, the way it holds itself. I don't need to see the fangs.

"Please," I say, my voice now hardly more than a whisper. "My name is Narissa Knight. I'm—

"We know who you are. We know exactly who, and *what*, you are."

"What do you mean, *what* I am?"

A thought strikes me and I shake my head.

"I'm not with them. I'm not with Blackwatch. I promise, I won't tell them about the other vampire. Neither will my friend. We won't say a thing about Styx. Please let me go."

CHAPTER 38

He steps forwards, now standing just a foot from the door. He's old in physical appearance and, I sense, in actual years. Older than Calin and Styx, I would bet my life. Although I'm not sure I'm going to get the chance to do that. Suddenly conscious of my exposed nakedness, I crouch down to cover myself.

"Please," I say again. "I will never speak of Styx again."

"Damien Styx is dead," he replies.

"Dead? How? What happened?"

Visions, like drunken memories, swirl in my mind. Once again, I see him looking at me. See the fear in his eyes. That was the last thing I can remember.

"Damien Styx was torn to death, as only a werewolf could do"

"Werewolf?" It can't just be Oliver who was hit on the head, although whether it's the old vamp or me who's barking, I have no idea. "What do you mean, werewolf?"

"We let you have your peace. We gave you our venom. And this is how you repay us." His voice is a hiss, like water fizzing on a hotplate.

"Please, I don't know what you're talking about."

"Conspiring with witches."

"Rey. What did you do to her? What did you do?"

"I'm the one who's asking questions. Tell me, which of the packs sent you?"

The questions keep coming but I can't process them. I can't process anything at all. It's like he's speaking to me through a blizzard.

"Fine then, have it your way."

The vampire turns on his heel and walks at pace away from me.

"Wait! Stop!" I scream, grabbing the bars. "I don't understand. Really, I don't. What am I doing here? What do you want with me?"

He's just on the edge of the shadows when he turns back and stares at me.

"I would enjoy your meal, if I were you, Ms Knight," he says, gesturing at the rotting meat. "It will be your last."

39

Calin

Of all the tricks to fall for. How could I not have seen it coming? I race back to London, the soles of my feet burning as I cover gravel and grass, tarmac and shingle. I cut across fields, through towns and villages. Not once do I pause. Yet, all the time, I know I will be too late. Styx had her. There was nothing I could do.

If I wasn't so set on ripping out his heart, I would have applauded his ingenuity, swapping out my phone for one with a dead battery. There was no way I could have known until I reached the hotel. The sound of Narissa's voice, screaming down the line—if I live a thousand more years, I swear I will still be hearing it.

I finally arrive back at my flat, to find it cordoned off

by police. Not vampires, or Blackwatch, but regular police.

"What's happened?" I ask. "What's going on?"

"Not sure at the minute, Sir, we're just gathering evidence, if you'd step back, please."

"But it's my home. I live here!"

His eyes widen a fraction. "Well, in that case, you can go over to the officer over there and give her a statement about where you've been for last twelve hours."

"I can what?"

Off to the right, a policewoman is looking at me. She goes to beckon me over with a simple nod, but I don't have time for this. I need to find Narissa. She has barely finished moving her head, when I am gone.

With my flat out of bounds, I have two options. Oliver's phone has rung dead all night, which doesn't bode well. Either I go to the Vampire Council, or to Blackwatch. As it's a human life in question, and with Styx being part of the Council, I choose the latter.

The Blackwatch organisation occupies a four-story house in Richmond. While the building itself is unimposing and of average size for these parts, rumour has it that there's a half-acre basement running from beneath it which houses, among other things, an armoury. I've occasionally been tempted to find out if there's any truth to this, but today is not the day. As it happens, I don't even need to enter the building. Standing outside, wearing a long trench coat with his phone pressed to his ear, is Jessop himself. He sees me and ends the call.

"Do you have any idea what's going on?" he asks. "Tell me you've got something."

Not what I was expecting, given that I'm the one who's come to him, hoping for information.

"I'm sorry? I'm not sure I know what you're talking about. I wanted to speak to Grey. Do you know where he is?"

"Oliver? Well, fingers crossed, he's out of surgery and not heading to ICU."

"Surgery? ICU? What happened? I've been out of London and out of contact."

"Honestly?" He sighs and rubs his temples. "I guess that figures. We got a call from him, about six last night, telling us we needed to get to an address, quickly. *Your* address, apparently. He said it was an emergency. All agents required."

He sighs again and reaches into his pocket, pulling out a packet of cigarettes. I clench my fist but wait for him to light up and take that first drag.

"Have you been to your place?"

I shake my head. "Only outside. Police were swarming all over."

"Probably best you didn't go in. Get a cleaning crew in there first. A good one. I've seen some shit in my time, but that…"

"What did you see? And why is Grey in hospital? Where's Narissa?"

"Narissa?" He lowers his cigarette and frowns. "What's she got to do with it?"

Shit. If he doesn't know, I'm not going to be the one to give him anything else.

"Sorry, she doesn't matter. Just tell me about Grey. And the flat. What did you find? What happened there?"

"What did we find? Well, Oliver on his last legs and a

bloody great werewolf, chomping its way through what turns out to be a member of your Blackwatch Council."

"A werewolf? In my apartment?"

"Yeah. So if you've got any idea how it got there, we'd very much like to know. Your lot are dealing with it now. Safe to say, Polidori did not sound happy. A werewolf. In London. Can you believe it? Never in all my days. I've seen them before, mind you. But here?"

No. No. I start pacing. I can hardly believe it, but I may have to. If Narissa wasn't in my apartment, but a werewolf was, there's only one inference to make, even if it is a huge leap of the imagination. Shit. The one thing that's needed to complete the transformation of a dormant werewolf is vampire venom. One tiny scratch would be enough to do it. Both times I fed from her, she refused to be scratched by me. Did she already know? Was I being played after all? She told me, after the Blood Bank fiasco, that her intention had been to infiltrate the vampires. Was this the final act of seeing it through? But then, what about her friend? Her upset was genuine as is, I believe, her relationship with Grey. There are too many unknowns for me to figure this all out right now. But one thing is certain: if a rogue werewolf kills a vampire—any vampire, let alone a member of the Council—there is going to be only one outcome. The question is, whether or not she deserves it.

"Where is the werewolf now?" I ask.

"Polidori has it, I assume. We grabbed Oliver and shut the door on the way out. You know how this works. We deal with the human side of things; you deal with the rest."

"Polidori?"

"He said he'd take care of it. I left two agents posted outside to wait for him to arrive. Apparently, someone had called the police, but we were able to pull rank and keep them away from the building for a while."

"Shit."

"Something wrong?"

"I'm not sure."

If Polidori has her, then there's only going to be one outcome.

"What hospital did they take Oliver to?" I ask, knowing full well that the only person who might be able to give me an eyewitness account could well be on an operating table.

"Portland Street. I'm heading there myself if you want a ride."

It's a nice offer. It genuinely is. For any human to volunteer to be in an enclosed space with a known vampire, shows character. But I'm faster on my own. As it is, I'm already on my way there before he probably even realises I'm gone.

40

It takes me less than five minutes to find Oliver. That's the good news. The bad news is they have pumped him full of painkillers. I can smell them flowing through his veins from the doorway. The man has been beaten black and blue. His left eye is swollen shut, and his bottom lip split so wide that I'm surprised his jaw didn't snap clean in two. Poor guy. Even after all the cleaning, plus the stench of the operating theatre, I can still smell Styx on him. The fact Grey is still standing is quite something.

A nurse fiddling with his IV bag looks up to see me in the doorway. "Who are you? There are no visitors allowed. You shouldn't be in here."

"I … I'm with the police," I lie.

Her scowl deepens. "You want to question him now? Does it look like he's up to it?"

"I'm sorry. Obviously, there was a misunderstanding."

"Yes, obviously."

Still mumbling my apologies and trying to work out

what to do next, I back out of the room and slip into the next one. The bed is occupied by an old man. He must have half a dozen wires attached to him, plus a drip going into his arm and a ventilator breathing for him. Even without the digital display, I can tell his heart is weak. But it's regular. That's good. Suddenly seeing a solution right in front of me, I unclip the lead that travels from him to the heart monitor. The room immediately fills with a warning siren, which is followed closely by a handful of nurses rushing in, including Oliver's.

Before they have a chance to blink, I'm out and back next door.

"Grey? Grey, can you hear me? It's Calin. I need to speak to you. Come on! Wake up man!"

Given all the swelling, it's tough to tell if he is even trying to open his eyes, but when his lips open slightly and he utters a hoarse croak, I'm almost certain he has heard me.

"Grey, try not to move, okay? Wiggle your fingers if you can hear me."

I see pain on his face, but he moves his fingers without the slightest hesitation.

"Okay … Okay … Grey, I need to know. Did she know what she was? Did she know she was a werewolf?"

I feel a total arsehole, disturbing a guy in complete agony, but I can't afford to get this wrong. If she has planned this all along—made up a story about her father so she could get close to the Council and start killing them—well then, she deserves everything that's coming to her. But if she didn't know and had no idea what effect venom would have on her. Well, in that case, one terrified young woman is about to come to an end that no innocent person deserves.

Another sound crosses his lips. It's rasping and weak.

"She didn't know. We didn't know. Save her."

"You're sure? You're sure she didn't realise?"

This time he nods. It's minuscule but causes all his features to crumple in agony.

"Save her," he says again.

"I will."

A moment later, I'm gone.

The problem is, saying you are going to save someone from execution and actually achieving it are two very different things. I should know. Before Polidori promoted me, I served time as a guard. Vampires have a lot of things to keep hidden, and I'm not just talking about grimoires. After the Blood Pact was signed, any major indiscretions led to death, or incarceration in the vaults beneath the Council's chambers. Vaults that are secured by vampire guards. No one gets in, or out, without authorisation. And now I need to get me in and two of us out.

There's only one way I'm going to stand any chance of managing it, and it's not going to be easy.

Narissa

I have no way of marking how many hours have passed. No phone to look at, not even any direct sunlight to judge the time of day. Every now and then, I hear noises. Sometimes it's laughter, but it's cold and cruel, maybe intended for me to hear. Then there are the screams—are there more like me here? But, for now, it's just me and the flies.

My thoughts keep circling back to Oliver. The way his head had slumped forwards. Did they get there in time to save him? Why don't I know? Why can't I remember?

In a corner of the cage, I found a blanket which I have wrapped around me, and the cold seems to have lessened. My body, despite its nakedness, is warm enough now. My mind, on the other hand … werewolf? The way the vampire spoke the word and the look he gave me. It just can't be possible. If werewolves existed, I would have known. Dad, Oliver, Rey, someone would have mentioned them at some point. But with the memories that have begun to creep back—the way everything changed when Styx scratched me—I'm starting to doubt my own sanity.

I kick at the meat, trying to disperse some of the flies, but they return almost immediately. I kick again. The cycle repeats. I'm not sure how long I have been at this when another sound catches my attention. It's coming from above. There it is again: a loud thud, followed by another.

"Well, this is it Narissa," I say out loud to myself. "You never did want to be ordinary. I'd say death-by-vampire is a tick on that list."

The noise grows louder still. Whatever or whoever it is, it's coming for me, of that I'm convinced. Pulling the blanket tighter around myself, I edge back into a corner, clenching a fist in readiness. Whatever they plan on doing, I'm not going quietly. And despite the pain in my chest and the feeling of emptiness that has all but consumed me, I'm more ready to fight than I've ever been in all my life.

There's another thud, and I drop the blanket. There's no way it's going to be anything other than a hindrance. Fuck it, I'll fight naked. Maybe it'll act as a distraction.

I hear approaching footsteps and the grating of metal hinges as a door opens. I find myself dropping into a crouch, knees bent, fingertips touching the cold, stone floor, as if preparing to spring at whatever's coming. A loud, guttural sound rises from the bottom of my throat. It seems more animal than human, but I don't care. I'm way past embarrassment now. But, as I push back onto my heels, ready to pounce, I hear his voice.

"Narissa? Narissa are you in there?"

"Calin? Calin!" All my strength and resolve evaporate as my knees give way, and I crumple to the floor.

"We need to get you out of here. Hold on a minute while I unlock this."

He's standing there, just outside my cell. Never before have I wanted so desperately to reach out and touch someone. Suddenly reminded of my nakedness, I pick up the blanket and wrap it back around myself. When I look up, he's still fiddling with the keys. From above us come angry yells.

"Can't you just break it open?" I ask, aware of the voices growing nearer by the second. "You're a vampire, for God's sake."

"So were the people who built this. And so are the people who are meant to stay locked inside. Just give me a minute!"

The sound of approaching footsteps would suggest we don't have a minute but, for once, I keep my mouth shut.

"There," he says, and the door swings open.

I race out, wanting to wrap my arms around him but knowing there's no time for that now.

"What the hell is going on?"

"There are guards," he tells me quickly. Even in the gloom, I can see the worry etched on his face. "Lots of them. There's no way we're going to be able to get through them with you like this."

"Like this?" I look down at the blanket, thinking he's asking me to take it off.

He shakes his head. "No, I mean as a human. The only way we can survive, is if you shift."

"Shift?"

"Turn wolf."

A new chill runs down my spine and I shake my head. "Calin, I'm not … I don't know how … I can't …"

"I know, I know," he says, resting a hand on my shoulder. "And we'll work it out later. We'll find the answers to all your questions, but for now you've *got* to do this."

I know from the tone of his voice that he's desperate. But become a wolf? How do I even try to do that? Do I stare at my hands and imagine them as paws? Do you call a werewolf's feet paws? Shit, if I don't even know that. How the hell am I expected to *shift*?

"I can't," I say again. "I'm sorry. I just don't know how. I don't know what I'm meant to do."

"It's all right," he says. "Just stay close and listen to everything I say. The only way we stand a chance of getting out of this is if you do everything I tell you."

42

It could be a scene out of a movie. One of those blockbuster, action ones that Oliver loves and Rey and I would go along to watch, just to keep him company. Calin walks ahead of me and we approach the stairs. The ceiling above us is thick with cobwebs. There's a heavy, iron, medieval-style light fitting bolted to the wall, which Calin yanks loose and hands to me.

"I don't know how much good it'll do," he says, "but keep your back to the wall and just keep swinging."

Great. Blind hope is what we're counting on here, although having something solid in my hands gives me a surprising amount of comfort, even if it is ridiculously naive. Coming at a vampire with some rusty bit of metal feels as much use as throwing pebbles at a raging lion.

The first two vampires we meet are in the stairwell.

"Get back!" Calin yells. Armed with a stake each, they are easily as big as him, but they're clumsy, and whatever it was they were expecting, it wasn't him. Before they can even blink, he has the stakes out of their hands and into their hearts. As their bodies topple forwards, I push myself back against the wall.

"Are you okay?"

I nod.

"Good, because there are going to be more. A lot more."

I always hate it when people sugar-coat the truth. I've always said, even as a kid, that I'd prefer to be given it straight, and then I can work out what to do from there. But, at this precise moment, a little sugar-coating wouldn't go amiss.

The staircase brings us out onto a long side-corridor that is flooded with daylight, which I wasn't ready for. To be fair, I think I'd be happier staying in the dark right now. But there's no way I can retreat or close my eyes. I have to face what's in front of us. There must be half a dozen vampires blocking our exit, each one armed, each one angry, although few seem to be looking at me.

"Sheridan? What the hell is going on? What are you doing with the girl?" one of them demands.

"Polidori told me personally to get her and take her to him."

"He's already seen the girl. My instructions are that no one gets in or out."

"Well, I guess there are different instructions for different pay grades."

The guard chews his lip. "Well, what about these guys?" He indicates the prone vamps that Calin must have subdued on the way down to me.

"Again, not my worry," Calin says. "Now, are you going to let me pass?"

Some of them have turned their attention to me. No

doubt they can hear the way my heart is pumping, probably fast enough to put me into cardiac arrest. But, for a moment, I think we've got it. I think they're going to let us go. Then the one in charge lifts his chin a fraction.

"Let's call Polidori, shall we? Just to check. I'd hate there to be any misunderstanding."

In a flash, Calin is on him, snapping his neck, before plunging a stake straight through his sternum. The others immediately spring into action.

"Get the girl!" one of them yells. The nearest vampire hesitates, throwing me an almost fearful glance. It's enough. Calin jabs the stake straight through his spine. Another one comes from the side. Once again, he's there to block him. The same thing happens a third time and then a fourth. They then start to coordinate their attack, and within a minute I'm pressed against the wall, Calin's back the only thing shielding me from the vampires that now have us cornered. While most of them continue to look at me, one stares at Calin.

"Why are you doing this, Sheridan?" he asks, his voice dripping with disgust. "Just hand over the mongrel and you'll get out of this alive. Plead insanity. Say you're in love. Whatever. You'll get away with just a couple of hundred years. Why would you risk your life over some worthless mutt?"

The rest don't seem so keen on conversation. They look like they would prefer to just rip my throat out, but as long as we're still talking, I'm still breathing. I just hope Calin's got some clever trick up his sleeve.

"It appears we're in a bit of a stalemate," he says, in a voice way calmer than makes sense in our situation. "You can't let me go, not after what I've done. I understand that. But then I can't let any of you live, not now that you've seen me here."

"There are five of us, and just one of you. What do you think you're going to be able to do?"

"Well, there were twelve of you but, to be honest, I guess I'm just waiting for a miracle."

"Yeah? We'll I'm tired of waiting."

Fangs flash, as he lunges towards Calin, who in turn strikes out with his arm and knocks him to the side. It's a good hit, but the other vampire is back on his feet in half a second and ready for another attempt. Two others join him, all going for Calin.

Naz! Naz, help me!

I hear her voice, so clear it's like she's standing there beside me and it's echoing around the walls.

Please don't leave me, Naz. Please!

How is it possible? How can I hear her so vividly?

I close my eyes and shake my head. When I open them again, more vampires have swarmed around Calin. That's why I'm hearing her voice. It's the same way I lost Rey. History is repeating itself: me standing helplessly by, unable to do anything to save the person who's risked everything for me. I couldn't do anything then. I couldn't save her. And now I'm going to lose him the same way. Unless I do something.

The vampires are looking at me, like they're worried. Like there's actually something to be afraid of. That's when I realise, I can change this. This doesn't have to be the same as Rey.

It's like a bolt of lightning ripping down my spine. The pain is excruciating, as it feels like every bone in my body is snapped in two. Half in disbelief, half in awe, I sense my vision altering, sharpening. My other senses are changing too. My hearing. My sense of smell. All magnified.

Calin! My eyes go to my friend, now inundated by attackers as he continues to try and beat them off. Without hesitation, I seize the nearest one in my jaws and toss him aside, feeling the crunch of his bones as I do so. I catch another and do the same with him and then another.

With the numbers against us decreasing, Calin is able to grab one himself although, even when he throws it dead to the ground, he still has a look of fear in his eyes.

He seems to be speaking to me, but I can't make out what he's saying. Realising this, he points down the corridor, to where a vampire is racing away. It takes only three bounds for me to land on his back and bring him down. I clamp my jaws around his neck and rip his head clean off.

Panting, I turn and see Calin, bent and dishevelled. Every other vampire is now dead.

Slowly, I pad towards him. I want to thank him. Thank him for getting me out of there. Thank him for killing his own kind to save someone he barely knows. But I have no words, just a deep, guttural growl. Still, I keep walking towards him. It's only when I'm right by his side that I notice he's holding the iron light fitting in his hand.

A moment later, the whole world goes black.

EPILOGUE

I'm woken by a jolting movement, as the car I'm in pitches and rolls across uneven ground. Trying to make sense of the situation, I blink my eyes open and lift my head, but as I sit up, a searing pain shoots through my skull.

"Jesus," I say, reaching up and gingerly touching the spot where the pain seems to be emanating from, only to find a large welt there.

"You're awake."

"Calin?"

"You've been out for some time. Sorry about that."

While I'm in the back of an impressively spacious four-by-four, Calin is sitting in the front, driving down a muddy track, apparently in the middle of nowhere.

"What the hell? Where are we going?"

I suddenly remember seeing Calin, holding the ironware.

"What the hell did you do to me?"

EPILOGUE

Apparently not noticing or not caring about my distress, he keeps his eyes forwards, infuriatingly calm.

"I apologise for hitting you. I just wasn't quite sure how to get you out otherwise. I figured that carrying an unconscious werewolf to the car would be a darn sight easier than trying to coax a conscious one to follow me."

"Unconscious ..." I stop myself. "Did you even try the other option?" I ask, still carefully probing my scalp.

"I will admit, I did not."

Not sure what I'm meant to say to this, I sink back into the seat. A werewolf. That's it then. I don't know how and I don't know why, but I can't deny it. I'm a werewolf, whatever that means.

For a while, we continue to travel in silence. I sense that he's allowing me time, the chance to process what I've just learnt. He must be having to make some adjustments himself, too. Still, there are things I need to know.

"Where are we going?" I ask again.

With all the questions I have, this seems the most important at the moment, particularly as we appear to be driving far from civilisation.

"Where is it you're taking me?"

I watch his eyes in the rear-view mirror as he considers his answer. Then, for the first time, they look up and meet mine.

"I'm taking you to your people," he says. "I think it is time you met the pack."

CURIOUS TO SEE WHERE EXACTLY CALIN IS TAKING Narissa? Want to know whether he will really choose her over his vampire brethren? <u>Grab you copy of Dark Destiny, Book 2 in the Dark Creatures Saga now!</u>

SCAN ME

Wondering how Calin became a vampire? Claim your collection of FOUR prequel novellas and discover why Calin's allegiance to Polidori is so strong? PLUS, get information on new releases and exclusive content.

NOTE FROM ELLA

First off, thank you for taking the time to read **Dark Creatures**, Book 1 in the Dark Creatures Saga. If you enjoyed the book, I'd love for you to let your friends know so they can also experience this action-packed adventure. I have enabled the lending feature where possible, so it is easy to share with a friend.

If you leave a review **Dark Creatures** on Amazon, Goodreads, Bookbub, or even your own blog or social media, I would love to read it. You can email me the link at ella@ellastoneauthor.com

Don't forget, you can stay up-to-date on upcoming releases and sales by joining my newsletter, following my social media pages or visiting my website www.ellastoneauthor.com

ACKNOWLEDGMENTS

First off thank you to Christian for his amazing covers for the whole series and Carol for her diligent editing.

To Lucy, Kath and all the alpha and beta readers who have helped shape this novel, I'd be lost without you.

And lastly, thank you to all of you readers out there for taking a chance on my book. I hope it has bought you as much joy reading it as it did for me writing it.